T0064449

The Empty
Pedestal
and Other Stories

THE EMPTY
PEDESTAL
AND OTHER STORIES

R.M. Rajgopal

PARTRIDGE
A Penguin Random House Company

To order additional copies of this book, contact
Partridge India
000 800 10062 62
orders.india@partridgepublishing.com

www.partridgepublishing.com/india

For My Parents

Illustrations by Ajit Ninan

CONTENTS

ACKNOWLEDGEMENTS

My father Prof. T.R.K. Marar who brought me up on a large and eclectic collection of books

My mother Indira Marar who encouraged me to read

Viju, my wife who provided me with encouragement, valuable criticism and support

My son, Arjun and my daughter, Uttara whose childhood escapades are caught in many of the stories

Ajai Malhotra who provided invaluable tips

Meenakshi Gopinath and Rajiv Mehrotra who purloined one of my stories and entered it in a National competition. Getting recognition there boosted my self confidence

And Manoj Menon who got the manuscript together in one document - no mean task, let me assure you.

I also wish to thank Poonam Jayarajan for an exemplary job of the cover design.

My very special thanks to Ajit Ninan for a brilliant job of the cover cartoon and three cartoons within the body of the book.

And last but not the least I am grateful to the erstwhile Indian Airlines whose almost perennially late flights gave me the time and space to write.

R.M.Rajgopal

FOREWORD
- THE EMPTY PEDESTAL

*T*his collection of short fiction has been written over a period of two decades.

The stories do not belong to any particular genre. They could vary from addressing issues of national import to dealing with the trivia of everyday life.

Having been written over a period of time some of the stories are dated and have to be read with this in mind.

This is a product of simple, straightforward storytelling to be read, enjoyed and pondered over.

As with much of short fiction each story is a snapshot. Yet the attempt is to make each as complete as possible.

In a sense the stories are a commentary on the India of today - its strengths, its weaknesses, its frailties, its eccentricities, its idiosyncrasies.

THE EMPTY PEDESTAL

The tension in the air is palpable. Feelings are running high. Dhani Ram is masterly at this, this strumming a mob skilfully into a high pitch of glaze-eyed emotion, a veritable Mark Anthony with his seductive words and the range and the quality of his voice. The scene immediately outside the gate is mildly chaotic, a swirling throng of moving bodies clad in pale-blue uniforms, Dhani Ram, similarly clad, standing on a stool at the centre of the circle, perched rather precariously I should think, as he orchestrates the crowd to chant in unison the word *chakka jaam*. And at a signal from him, the crowd seats itself in unison, cross-legged on the road outside. Watching from within, separated from the throng outside by thick bars and even thicker cement, I am not unduly perturbed. This is the fourth evening in a row that this very show outside the gate has been enacted, a prelude to the fourteen-day notice to strike work given in support of demands that the owners have refused to even consider. I know for sure that the sequence isn't going to last any more than twenty minutes for even Dhani Ram's charismatic persona isn't substitute enough for the cup of hot tea waiting at home or maybe the glass of warm arrack at the nearby adda, for the winter sun by this time in the evening is well on its way down, and soon the nip in the air is going to start to bite. And the cold, damp, hard, grey-brown tarmac would add to the discomfort.

It is all a part of the build-up for D-day. Dhani Ram realizes well enough that he has us by our privates, for business is booming and the loss of profits would be daunting indeed if a prolonged stoppage of work did take place. The situation has reached a firm impasse, both sides unrelenting, the negotiation process having got severed even before it ever got seriously started. I wonder to myself how all this is going to end up, what my bosses have exactly on their minds, for they look to be as adamant as Dhani Ram can at times be intemperate. Neither can win, it looks to me, and neither is prepared to lose either. I see difficult times ahead for me, for I am part of the go-betweens, a tiny, inconsequential part but a part nevertheless, and as I watch the froth coalesce slowly but surely into a boil, I realize that I will have to be in the thick of it soon enough. And I doubt that I can make any kind of cogent impression on Dhani Ram despite, at a personal level, being able to relate to him with a degree of closeness that has often surprised me, a strange bonding, the two of us, so different in temperament, in our world views, and not merely that—placed in positions that are almost naturally adversarial.

The full-throated shouting goes on, rising to a deafening crescendo every couple of minutes, the sound echoing behind me off the tall, thick walls of the factory building, making the five hundred strong squatters sound more like a couple of thousand. Another ten minutes at best, I tell myself, and then I can phone inside for my colleagues to come out and occupy their seats in the row of buses lined by the side of the road, all the drivers presently crowded into the one parked closest to the scene of action, taking in the free entertainment.

I fail to notice the dark-blue van at first as it crawls up the road towards the gate and parks itself in the centre, blocking passage, only yards away from the outer fringes of the seated assemblage. It is only when the contents of the van spill out, wearing khaki shorts and shirts, stout lathis under their armpits and carrying sturdy, triangular shields made of cut bamboo poles woven together with stout jute twine, that I become aware with a start of what is happening. Without ado, the new arrivals move purposefully in, trampling over those seated on the ground, swinging their sticks in brief, forceful, staccato arcs in front of them, connecting with shoulders, with necks, with the behinds of heads. *Thud. Thud.* They stride through the crowd, some prostrate from the blows, other rising to their feet in consternation.

Dhani Ram, suddenly aware of the melee behind him, turns around and attempts to clamber off the stool. He is unsuccessful at first as the crowd in its confusion, hems him in. And he seems to be the target the khaki-clad ones are seeking, for they head straight for him. Even as he finally manages to climb down, he is distinctly identifiable. As he instinctively covers the rear of his head with clasped palms and turns around into a defensive, crouched posture, the blows rain down. It is all over in a few minutes, and as the crowd disperses clutching arms and heads in agony, what remains unmoving are scores of chappals strewn around, and Dhani Ram, prostate on the ground, lying strangely twisted on his side, his palms still clasped in instinctive self-defence over his head.

The crowd has scattered. Most have taken to their heels. The few who have their wits about them, spotting their fallen colleague, rush to his aid. I can see the fear on the faces, can sense their terror. Unsure of what to do, I run towards the nearest phone to report the happenings to those waiting inside.

* * *

It was a mere week into this, my very first job, that I first encountered Comrade Dhani Ram. A charge sheet had to be handed out, a reprimand to someone caught in sound slumber during the night shift. He stalked in, an air of aggressiveness about him, into my spartan, airless chamber located adjacent to the room where the workers punched their attendance cards as they came in. Accompanying him was the intended recipient of the missive, Dhani Ram, there to provide the recipient with moral support perhaps. And as I took out the letter, Dhani Ram insolently snatched it from my hand. After reading it word for word, he signalled to his companion that it was in order for him to receive it. Which the companion did, sullenly.

Dhani Ram continued to sit in the room as his companion walked out. When we were alone, he looked me straight in the eye. Unblinking. Sizing me up for the stripling that I was.

'Have you ever worked a night shift?' he asked me.

'No,' I replied.

'Do you know what it is like,' he continued, 'keeping awake all night when it is natural for the rest of the world to sleep?

Not merely keeping awake but labouring, labouring hard? Do you know how much heat those machines generate? Have you any real idea of how hot it is in there? Have you ever spent more than five minutes at a time in there? Yes, you can say that he has broken the rules. I don't deny that. And I am sure you will punish him for it. But rules are not all. And charge sheets and punishments don't solve problems. They only add to them. And create bitterness. Remember that.' A small-made, spare man, with grey-black hair, piercing eyes, round black plastic spectacle frames. A lean face, thin to the point of gauntness yet his visage mobile with emotion when he spoke. I nodded at him, partly, I confess, in genuine empathy.

'A cup of tea?' I asked him.

That was the beginning. Perhaps what drew us together was my respect for his intellect, for his deep understanding of whatever it was that he believed in. Outmoded perhaps, inconsonant with the changing times, incompatible with the inevitable forces of the free market. Yet what was important to me was that his belief was fervent, his convictions genuine. Which is why it became a ritual of sorts, this weekly cup of tea and conversation, of verbal sparring, of often intense debate, of each attempting to understand the other a little better. I learnt a lot from him. Of that, there is no doubt in me. More than anything else, I learnt to empathize with the essential human condition, an empathy that has helped me both in intellectual and emotional terms to bridge the deep divide that separates my milieu from his. And as I sit and stare out pensively at the unruly grey sea from my office on the sixteenth floor of this building on Cuffe Parade, I acknowledge to myself that I owe him a lot. For what I have made of my life, for what I am now. And when I look back across time, I am grateful.

* * *

It is a solemn function. The local MLA presides. Money has been spent unstintingly. The shamiana is sparkling new; the carpet underfoot is clean and soft to the touch. The garlands of fresh marigold glow a soft orange-yellow. The entire factory is assembled, and that includes the owners themselves. The atmosphere is one of hushed, expectant silence.

On the dais, the VIPs sit behind a long table. By the side of the dais is a structure shrouded with a white silk curtain.

First the unveiling, then the speeches. The MLA pulls at the drawstring. The curtains part. An amazing resemblance. Dhani Ram come to life, his face, his shock of thick hair, even his round-framed spectacles. A remarkable likeness. He stares at the crowd, sightless.

The speeches start. Each on the dais comes up by turn. Solemn phrases, praise for the man that was. Good words about his intellect, his sagacity, his qualities as a leader. And voices choke with emotion as the dastardly incident is mentioned, a result of misguided, overreaching, spur-of-the-moment, impulsive action. An enquiry is on, the findings expected shortly.

After each speech, a garland of marigolds is placed around Dhani Ram's neck by the speech-giver. I am sure that I am imagining this, but do I catch a hint of a sardonic smirk on Dhani Ram's face? Maybe that is how the sculptor captured him in stone. It may be, again, that he is smiling to himself somewhere. The irony of it all. I am unsure.

The program over, the crowd departs, silent and solemn. I am one of the last to leave. Standing by my side is Dhani Ram's successor, a plump, genial, quick-witted man who, just a month previously, after barely a week of parleys, had signed on the piece of paper that helped conclude matters peaceably. No strike, no stoppage of work. No sales lost. And no profits either. A practical, earthy person, not one given to stubborn stands and unshakeable beliefs. How could he, I ask myself, after what has happened? It is as if he has read my thoughts. Next to the pedestal upon which Dhani Ram's bust reposes is a large blob of cement fallen on the ground, left there by the masons who, working to a tight deadline, had to wind up their work and leave rather hastily. 'That,' my companion tells me, pointing to the blob of cement, 'is the empty pedestal. For the next one who creates trouble. And is turned into a statue in stone. I have a wife and three children to look after, sahib.'

* * *

THEY LISTENED

*P*eter Osborne's romanticism manifested itself in many ways. In his aloof lifestyle, in his brooding Byronic looks—striking though slightly greyed with age—in his sensitive deep-set eyes, in the poetry that he sometimes wrote though seldom of late. It was evident yet again in the bouts of self-pity that he often went through, for they almost always took on hues of the mildly melodramatic. His current mood was one of despondency, bordering on shades of despair. Despondency at this uncaring world, at his own useless self, at the life he lived, at this accursed city that he found himself in, and most of all, at this slightly off-track hotel that paid him so generously—employment for people of his genre wasn't very easy to come by—and thus bound him to a way of life that he had come to despise. His state of existence was like the Simon and Garfunkel number, he said to himself. People hearing without listening. Not that he cared much for newfangled music. A cacophony of assorted sounds, shrieking voices, deliberately off-tune instruments—or so it seemed to him—with no rhythm, no subtlety, no grace.

Contemporary music for him had ended in the early sixties, when he had discovered the piano and its route to musical purity. After that, it had been the piano for him and little else in all this while. Every evening like clockwork—except Mondays, his day off—Peter thumped away at the piano in the obscure corner of the hotel's only restaurant and not a soul to listen to him, much less appreciate or applaud. He often wondered whether to the hotel's management, he was rather like a part of the restaurant's decor, to be equated with the furniture, the chandeliers above, and the slightly soiled carpet underfoot. Playing to an unresponsive, wooden audience can be terrible for your confidence. Playing to an audience, half of whom didn't even notice that you were there, was even worse. It made you ponder about your very existence, for the lack of meaning in the situation was debilitating. It made Peter feel an emptiness that was disconcerting, an emptiness that had timelessness about it, for time itself seemed to stand still as one dreary day followed the other in grey, colourless progression. Yet the pay was good, the accommodation was reasonable, and not many hotels needed solo pianists. So there he was, adjusting rather well in the overall to the vacuousness of his life, except for these moody currents that wafted by him just once in a while, filling him with pangs of a lonely melancholy.

But what troubled him the most was the thought of what his circumstances might have done to his music. Peter often wondered to himself whether his playing had rusted. Were his fingers as nimble as they had always been, flying over the keys, light yet firm? Was he as flawless as before? Or was he ever so slightly off-key? He had no way of judging, and he didn't trust his own ears, knowing fully well how narcissistic he was about his own music. This vestige of self-doubt was even more difficult to live with than was the melancholy of his existence. He pined for the good old days back in Calcutta when his audiences were connoisseurs of the kind of music he played, where he couldn't afford the smallest slip, for well-trained ears would catch on in a trice. The silent yet ever-present demand for excellence from the discerning, involved audience used to bring out the best in him. Sadly for him, it was not so here in Delhi where, forget being discerning—the audiences just weren't interested. He was hired, he supposed, for the groups of tourists from abroad who flocked to the city at most times of the year, for whom music and a restaurant went together. Every once in a very long while, there was a smattering of applause from one or the other of these visiting denizens at a piece he knew he had played particularly well. But that was every once in an awfully long while, and to the performing artiste that Peter essentially was, the intervals were too far apart and the applause too subdued. This surely wasn't what he deserved at this late stage in life, over forty years of music behind him and the three-score figure of age not so far away!

That Saturday evening in late September was as usual. A crowd of touring Italians had come in around eight, a full two dozen of them. A noisy lot, to say the least, dressed in clothes that seemed to be a special signature for touring the country, baggy psychedelic trousers and even baggier round-necked cotton shirts that sagged to well below the hipline, slightly scruffy sports shoes probably shiny white when they were brought but now stained a uniform grey brown. Excited voices were punctuated with loud laughter, the voices getting louder and the laughter a shade raucous as the evening progressed and vast quantities of beer went down throats parched from a long day walking around

Delhi's sundry forts, tombs, and monuments. Peter was in his assigned corner for the four hours of playing that was required of him from eight until midnight. He was permitted a half hour off in between for a cup of tea and some respite. Strange, he said to himself, that he even thought of the break as respite—even five years back, an intermission hadn't been something to look forward to quite so much, for he loved his music so.

The baby grand, in Peter's reckoning, was ever so slightly off tune. Only a really discerning ear such as his could pick up the slight flaw. He had tried to get it set right more than once, but repeated attempts at tuning hadn't made any appreciable difference. Delhi didn't seem to have anyone who quite knew how to—little wonder, considering the sparse piano population in the city. Pianos that were played on. Not those used as drawing room adornment, a convenient perch for those exquisite pieces of Waterford. In his native Calcutta, there were half a dozen guys who could have done the tuning blindfolded!

Calcutta. The city was an obsession with him. Not as it was now, seedy, with its crowded streets, its unpainted buildings, its devastating slums, and its omnipresent stench. He hadn't been back there for over ten years, and he didn't want to, for today's reality might very well cost him his dearly held image of the fifties, a graceful place where life moved at an indolent metre, where the brown sahib oh-so-British boxwallahs set the pace, where the clubs were still grand and flourished with crowded evenings, good music, and graceful dancing, where a leisurely evening on Park Street meant an excellent shrimp cocktail and a steak done just right, preceded by a scotch and soda and washed down with a mug of very cold beer, where a jacket and tie even in hot, unbearably sweaty May would nary raise an eyebrow. He had no desire to go back. Most of his relatives had left long back for the Down Under, now comfortably ensconced in Melbourne and Sydney and Perth. The few stragglers who stayed behind were either in old people's homes or were thoroughly Indianized with children named Vikram and Arjun and Joya. He knew that he didn't belong in the new Calcutta and that neither did the city belong to him. Come to think of it, he said to himself, he belonged to nowhere in particular. He wondered once in a while of what would become of him as the years crept on him, slowly but inexorably. Maybe he would himself go to Australia—he had his only living siblings, two sisters, married and comfortable in Perth. Maybe he would find himself in an old folks' home like many others, ever in wait for letters that seldom arrived. Maybe he would die suddenly, and that possibly would be best way to go, for he hated the idea of being a burden on anybody. Peter shook himself out of his reverie as he started on his next piece, for audience or no, he was disciplined about his playing.

He was, as always, engrossed with his music whilst he played and was slightly startled, therefore, at the tap on his shoulder as he ended the piece with a flourish—a flourish superfluous perhaps with none listening and none to applaud. Turning in his chair, he saw that it was Kishen Chand, the restaurant's head waiter, a piece of hotel stationery in his hand.

In many ways, Kishen Chand and the restaurant were strangely alike: both a little past their prime, both slightly frayed at the edges, yet retaining, resolutely, shreds of a dignity that in the restaurant's case the slightly garish new decor and in Kishen Chand's the faintly ridiculous, stylized costume that he was decreed to wear couldn't take away. Both were relics of the Raj—quaint and a bit out of step with the times, especially in Delhi where, despite being British India's capital for well nigh half a century, the colonial hangover didn't persist, except in odd ways such as the local habit of never using fingers to partake of food when eating out. Not that this faint flicker of the Raj was ever transformed into any serious degree of table manners. A belch was still the best way of expressing appreciation at a particularly satisfying repast. Elbows off the table, eat with your mouth shut, don't talk with your mouth full, don't reach across the table— none of these parental admonitions of Peter's childhood applied in any way. Colonial hangover or no, Kishen Chand was indisputably dignified in the grace of his mien, in the thick shock of silver hair combed neatly off his brow, in his trimmed moustache, a moustache that had character—unlike the wimpy ones some people seem to sprout nowadays—in his still straight back and in his steady, purposeful gait. His English, grossly incorrect in pronunciation, grammar, and usage yet must have been otherwise at some time in the past, well complemented the pidgin Hindustani of the white sahib. A relic like himself, Peter often thought. Yet it would do some of the younger waiters a whale of good to emulate Kishen Chand even a part of the way. Not for him the sneaked beedies smoked surreptitiously in the stretch of passage between the restaurant and the kitchen, nor the idling around and gossiping, sometimes even within earshot of customers. He was efficient and courteous, good-humoured and self-effacing. Peter got on well with Kishen Chand. Often when he sat down late at night for dinner in a corner of the restaurant as he was permitted to, Kishen Chand, if he was around, obliged him with an extra-large helping of whatever was served. Not that Peter was a big eater; it was the thought that mattered, he supposed.

The Italians had emptied out of the place, and all that were left behind were three or four groups of tourists of sundry national denomination, a quieter lot, concentrating on what was on the table before them with a fervour born out of hunger and thirst after a tiring day of sightseeing. The restaurant had quietened down and thankfully so, thought Peter as he enquired of Kishen Chand what the matter was. Kishen Chand handed over the piece of paper to him, and as he glanced at it, Peter was incredulous. No, it couldn't be. But yes, it was! Three requests, two of them favourite pieces of his. *Tales from the Vienna Woods*, *The Blue Danube*, *Für Elise*. Peter couldn't believe his eyes. 'Which table?' he enquired of Kishen Chand.

'Number nine in the right hand side,' he replied.

The woman wore a pale-blue sari, the man a deep maroon shirt. Not young by any means but not old either. Late thirties is what he would put them at. Neatly turned out, but not flamboyant. Looked the quiet sort, though for the life of him he couldn't figure out why they had chosen this hotel and, more than that, this restaurant, both obscure at best. May be it was the food, which in Peter's reckoning was good, especially the so-called continental variety, despite shades of native spicing creeping in once in a while.

'Staying here?' he enquired of Kishen Chand, who was still standing near him.

'I don't think so,' Kishen Chand replied. 'I seeing no room keys with them.'

As he looked towards them, she caught his eye. A half smile traversed the corners of her mouth in acknowledgement of the requests. Peter inclined his head ever so slightly, indicating both receipt and acquiescence. This was serious. The first time ever in the three years that Peter had been here. Requests, actually. He steeled himself mentally as he seated himself a little firmer and straighter and started to play.

And play he did with the passion and the fire of old, tiny droplets of sweat breaking out on his brow just below his hairline as his fingers raced over the keys, his hands moving swiftly as he went through the paces, missing not a beat, not a note out of place, finishing with a flourish, well deserved this time as he looked up expectantly for applause. So what if only the two of them clapped? After three years of near drought, even a drizzle felt like a torrent. Peter smiled and bowed his head, this time a little more pronouncedly in acknowledgement of their appreciation. He went on to the next two numbers and then to two more of his own choice that he knew by instinct they would like. Polite applause followed each time. He could well have carried on, but it was time for his break. Time for a cup of piping hot tea and a couple of biscuits. He was a creature of habit. Too late in life now to change.

Melancholy was something he was quite used to in the loneliness of his existence. And boredom. Joy came but rarely, and Peter didn't quite know how to handle it. The joy of playing to someone who listened, the joy of being appreciated. The ecstasy of the music in itself. The sweat on his brow was a sure sign, he said to himself, that he had played well. Sweat on his brow after a long time. Too long, by Jove. Lost in his thoughts, he almost scalded his tongue with the first sip of the boiling hot tea that he had been served. Had they discerned the slightly flawed tuning of the instrument? Probably not, for they had been seated some distance away and the restaurant, though not unduly noisy sans the Italians, was not entirely quiet either. Who were they? he wondered. Had he played well enough to tempt them to come back? Maybe. When he got back after his half hour of rest, the couple had departed. Nevertheless, his spirits felt elevated and he enjoyed himself, playing the rest of the evening through. Kishen Chand was agreeably surprised when he asked for a beer with his meal that night—something that he did rarely, if ever at all.

Peter was back in his room well past midnight. The room was small, rectangular, with a narrow bed, a clothes cupboard built into the wall and a rather threadbare carpet that was fraying in odd spots, the grey mosaic, unswept and unpolished for years, peeping out from underneath. A faded print of an old Rajput miniature was framed and hung on the wall above the headboard. A small writing desk and chair were placed on the side; two more chairs and a low coffee table crowded the area between the bed and the wall. A small window with rather grimy panes looked out on to the hotel backyard and beyond it on to the grounds of a government office building. The room had a tiny bathroom attached. Not the most cheerful of abodes, and not the most edifying of views. The saving grace was the air-conditioning, part of the central system that catered to the hotel, for it helped Peter cope with Delhi's ghastly summer heat—he surely couldn't have survived without it.

After a shower and a change into nightclothes, Peter picked up the paper that he had weighed down with an ashtray on the table near his bed. He opened a new notebook that he pulled out of one of the shelves in his cupboard and, with a neat, precise hand, wrote down the titles of the three compositions that he had been requested to play that day.

For the next six days of that week, Peter peered often around the dimly lit restaurant. No, no sign of them. Yet it seemed as if the quality of his playing had upped a notch almost as if by itself, perhaps in anticipation of the day they might be back and more requests come his way. He seemed to concentrate more too, and to be a little more thoughtful in the selection of his pieces than he was before.

And yes, Saturday week they were there again. He didn't notice them coming in, and the first indication of their presence was Kishen Chand's tap on his shoulder as he finished a piece. This time he spread the numbers over forty-five minutes of playing, filling the rest of the time with his own selection. Peter enjoyed himself immensely, the sweat on his brow again a sure sign of both his joy and the quality of his playing. Beer at dinner time, leaving Kishen Chand wondering. Even Peter's appetite seemed to have improved, Kishen Chand noticed. No leftovers on his plate.

For the next three weeks, the Saturday night routine continued like clockwork. The thought of strolling over to their table at break time, introducing himself, making conversation, didn't occur to Peter. Yes, the quality of the requests that came his way did convince him that whoever it was that made them—the gentleman or the lady—knew music and knew it well. The diversity was amazing. Of the twelve so far he had to turn down two, not knowing how to play them. Which is what gave him all the more joy for if they were as knowledgeable as they looked to be; the fact that they liked his music meant that despite his apprehensions, he had not rusted. Not one bit, probably.

It was the fourth Saturday after the first, and it was already well past eight thirty. They were normally punctual, almost to the minute. Where were they? He looked often towards the entrance, but there was no sign of them. A quarter to nine, nine o'clock. Peter's anxiety grew. He could feel his playing getting slightly ragged— thank heavens no one in the place was listening with any keenness. At break time, the tea he normally so enjoyed tasted pallid. The biscuits remained untouched. He had to drag himself back to the piano when the half hour elapsed, and even then his playing was desultory. No beer with dinner, and he picked at his food. He didn't sleep very well either, waking up at first light and pottering around his room, feeling that nagging tiredness that hits you behind your eyes when you haven't had your full night's quota.

The week went by in a slow tedium, the audience as faceless and disinterested as ever. Saturday evening, and Peter's tension grew. He kept glancing at his watch every couple of minutes as the hour approached half past eight. Eight thirty-five, eight forty. Still no sign of them. It was almost a quarter to nine when he had given them up, and when he hadn't looked anxiously at the entrance for a while, that Kishen Chand's now familiar tap brought him back to the present. There they were at their usual table, the steward hovering around, engrossed in discussing between them some finer point of the menu. Peter's spirits soared. He settled down to an hour of non-stop playing, well over fifteen minutes into his break time—the first time that he had transgressed into his recess in many a year. After a hiatus of fourteen days, the feeling was exhilarating.

Maybe they had been musicians like him in their youth, playing as he did when he began, simply for the purity of the joy that he experienced through music. Unlike him, to whom music became both a lifetime's obsession and a livelihood, they must have moved on to other things that made more sense when one considered the serious issue of having to earn a decent living. Maybe they had lived abroad for many years and were used to quality performances, in which case he felt complimented because they seemed to like his playing. Maybe they were old Calcuttans recently come to Delhi where the kind of music he played was next to impossible to come by, a chance visit to the restaurant provoking nostalgia. Anyway, whoever they were, he was glad that they came, grateful for their applause, thankful that at least they listened. Listened, unlike all the rest of the folks who mostly didn't even realize he was there and, even if they did, didn't think he merited more than a cursory glance, or at best treated his music as a pleasant backdrop to the restaurant's ambience. His *music*, if you please. At least the two of them listened.

It was that in between season that could be labelled spring, somewhere near the end of Delhi's winter. The first flowers were in bloom. The weather was so perfect that both the damp, grey, cold days of January and the searing heat of May seemed an improbable fantasy; March, when the tourist season peaked each year until it tapered off barely a month later. Peter remembered that Saturday because it was Holi, a festival he particularly disliked. He was a fastidious man, and to be daubed with colour that took a week's vigorous scrubbing to get rid of wasn't his idea of fun. Downright barbaric, he felt. He normally shut himself up in his room the whole day and emerged only well past four in the evening, for by then the effects of the delirium that Holi seemed to inject in the average citizen, turning him ever so slightly savage for the duration of the morning, would have worn off and things would be back to some semblance of normality; except of course for hair temporarily dyed in vigorous bright colours and faces rather like at the commencement of a Red Indian War dance, or so Peter imagined.

That Saturday they didn't come, but after four in a row, that was forgivable. Holi's travails can be exhausting. A week passed, and they weren't there the next Saturday either. It didn't bother Peter much because it had happened before. Yet something niggled at him. *Never mind*, he told himself, *this has happened before*. They would be there the following weekend. But they weren't. Three Saturdays in a row was decidedly unusual. Peter began to miss them. And terribly too. During all those six months, the five performing days between Saturdays had been to Peter so many practice sessions, honing up his playing for the day they would come. Now he wasn't sure if they would ever come again. The drudgery, the joylessness, the seeming lack of meaning in his existence began to seep back into his consciousness. What could he do but hope and wait? But no. A whole month passed. Peter's playing was almost disinterested, and he was grateful for the fact that no one seemed to be particularly interested in him.

It took him full six weekends to come to terms with their absence. And his final acceptance of the reality caused him pain that seemed to know no end. It was well into summer by then, and the weather, he felt, only added to his general misery. He seriously began to think of retirement, but where could he go to? Perhaps Australia was, after all, the best bet. His sisters were more than willing to receive him; at least that that was what they said in their letters. Maybe their outlook would be different when confronted with the fact that his going there was a reality. It also meant to him a swallowing of his pride, a final acceptance of the fact that however well he played, however good he thought he was, his aspirations had come to naught. He would remain forever an obscure pianist, a restaurant performer, which was the worst that could possibly happen to a musician of his calibre. *Well*, he said to himself, *there is tomorrow to think about all this.* It was time for him to start.

When Peter went down, along with his normal music book he carried a notebook that he took out of his clothes cupboard. As he sat down at the piano, he opened it. He glanced at the long list of numbers inscribed neatly on the pages and said to himself, *Might as well start with Austria*. The home of Europe's music. And *Tales from the Vienna Woods* flowed as his hands moved effortlessly over the keys. And some of the people in the restaurant didn't notice him at all. And some heard him, probably. But none listened.

* * *

A Genuine Blonde

*T*he bungalow is large, gracious. It has a wide veranda that spans its frontage, with a floor of dark wood. At one end of the veranda is an easy chair framed in solid Burma teak. The chair has extra long arms and a broad seat of finely woven cane that curves gently upwards, the type that you can sprawl on gracelessly, legs akimbo on the arms, a restful haven for a lazy, tepid afternoon. There are more cane chairs placed in each half of the veranda, pale cream ones with a bunch of red squares clustered into large diamonds at the centres of their backs. The two ceiling fans, one for each half, still turn and noiselessly too, for they are sturdy ones that had come in on a slow ship from England over sixty years ago; Sir K. P. Chandy was not ever one to compromise on quality. And the knight of the empire is still very much a part of the house that he had built as he looks down from within the large framed photograph placed above the lintel of the door through which one entered the house.

He wears a tweed jacket and the broad striped tie is knotted in a Windsor. The clothes that he's dressed in are just so—ought to be, for the ICS was always particular about what it wore, trained as they were into an Englishness that after a while came to them naturally, colour of skin notwithstanding. It was reflected in their food habits, in the way they spoke the English language, in their gait, and in their demeanour. It was most pronounced, of course, in the decidedly strong views that they came to possess, of how the world ought to be. And the bungalow reflected all of this in a natural, wholesome, Macaulayian way. You could see and feel it in the way in which the house was shaped and built, the way it was brought to life, the furniture, the furnishings, the paintings on the walls, the cutlery, the crockery, where a claret glass was not to be confused with the one used to serve port in, where each form of liquor had its own crystal decanters, no vulgar bottles. A tea cosy over the teapot was still the norm, no flasks of steel or plastic. And it persisted in the manner in which meals were still served, in the way Vincent set the table, starched, tasselled, napkins of thick cotton in soft shades of pastel, the gleaming cutlery, the pale rose Johnson dinner service that was the norm for daily use, the Spode stowed away for the special occasion.

It was the Spode that Leila was arranging that evening with such care, for the occasion was indeed special. Special in more than one way. It was Sanjay's first time home in over three years. He ought to be arriving in an hour at the very latest, the journey up the ghat roads from Coimbatore off a flight that landed at four in the evening ought not to take more than three hours.

She had been confused more than anxious or irritated when she had received Sanjay's mail, out of the blue indeed, to announce that he was getting married. What had been the hurry, she wondered, why could he not have waited and had a proper ceremony and everything? Now even a reception didn't make sense; the event was half a year back into time. She had planned a small dinner that would make do; close friends and whatever relatives could be rustled up. But he is coming home, and really, Leila's joy knows no bounds. She only hopes Penelope wouldn't be overly tired, what with the long journey and the transits and the car ride at the end of it.

'Be careful,' she says to Vincent, 'this stuff can't be replaced if you break any of it.'

Vincent, small, dark, gray-haired, plump, nods acknowledgement and goes about the task of laying the table, she at the head, the two of them on either side of her. The china glitters, and the Sheffield gleams as she turns away and walks down the corridor to check if all is well with their bedroom. Everything is in place including the fresh roll of toilet paper. That was what had given her the most trouble; getting good branded stuff had taken her all the way to Ooty, an hour's drive away. She had bought a few extra rolls; though the two of them weren't going to be with her for long enough, Penelope wanted to get in as much of the country as she could. It was her first time out to India.

It is nearly dark as she steps onto the veranda to switch on the lights outside. As she turns to come back in, she looks up at the visage of her father, and is it the fading light playing tricks with her eyes, or can she see a hint of a smile on his face as if to say, 'Full circle, isn't it, Leila? Look at you with an English rose for a daughter-in-law, now who would have expected that?' It is as if the last fifty years of so-called freedom had been worth their while, the stoicism with which she had adjusted to the changing times where she could only look back with nostalgia at her childhood and the years immediately thereafter. Anachronistic, those times, if you looked at the context of today. Vindication, then, in a sense of the life that she had lived, which perhaps is why her father seemed to smile to himself, as she did to herself.

As she switches on the lights in the drawing room, it is Ravi that she looks at, enclosed in a small rectangular steel frame on the low bookshelf in the far corner. She is next to him in the photograph, both of them shoulder to shoulder and facing slightly sideways. And she is prim and so obviously self-conscious, staring wide-eyed into the camera. A pity that they had but a short time together, just a few fleeting years before the tumble that his jeep took traversing a steep bend on the estate that he managed, took him away from her and from Sanjay forever. Which is why this had always been her home, tending to her father until he too had taken leave of her a few years back leaving her to plod on, alone and lonely. She and Vincent and Mary and this sprawling old place. Yet she loved the house so, loved the manner in which everything about it was planned and preserved, every bit of it. Just desserts, Penelope's coming into the family. Need she say more!

She waits, eager in anticipation for the headlights of the car to shine through the grills of the gate as it drives up the sloping road that ends at the house. Sanjay, of course, knows every bit of the surroundings for though at boarding school for most of his childhood and then to college and hostel in Delhi soon after, he had grown up there, spent all his vacations there. And she knew that he loved these hills with their cloud-wrapped peaks, the tea gardens that wreathed the valleys, a little England almost, transplanted so neatly five thousand miles eastwards.

It is almost half past seven, and night has set in fully when she hears the drone of a car engine. Minutes later, headlights trace an uneven pattern through the gate. Vincent has heard the vehicle approaching and is at the gate, opening it to let the car in. Sanjay steps out, tall and slim, and he is wearing a T-shirt in dark maroon and tan slacks. Penelope follows. What strikes Leila in that instant of her first glimpse of her is her hair, a pale straw-yellow that has a luminescence about it, pulled back tight over her forehead in a ponytail. And the colour is striking even in the half-light of the veranda, the bulbs at that time of the evening being low on voltage. And Leila is reminded of Rapunzel and of the princess in Rumpelstilskin and of the many fairy tales of her childhood.

Leila steps forward to hug them by turn. She shows them to their bedroom at the far end of the corridor that runs down the middle of the house, and she is happy. Happy with Sanjay being here, and Penelope. Happy too at the thought of Papa, of how happy he would have been to have seen for himself the fairness of her skin, the pale gold of her hair. And her hair shimmers at dinner time, freshly shampooed and blow-dried, unloosened and framing her face as she tucks in with gusto into the rice and mutton curry that is served, using her fingers as does Sanjay, leaving the gleaming Sheffield untouched. There is no awkwardness; it is as if it was meant all along that the three of them would be together as they are, and Leila is delighted, her eyes brimming as she looks at each of them in turn.

She won't let them sit up and converse for too long after the meal for she knows that they must be exhausted, the long journey and lack of sleep. She persuades them to retire, and as they move towards the bedroom, she enquires of their preference of beverage for the morning. Both of them want tea, even Sanjay, an inveterate consumer of strong coffee in the days before he went to England. Seven in the morning is agreed, and good nights are exchanged.

Leila is asleep the instant she lies down, a combination of exhaustion and contentment.

She is up at first light and is in the kitchen at a quarter to seven, helping Vincent to brew the tea. Darjeeling. Cost an arm and a leg, but so what? The tea pot is covered with a flannel cosy, the tea tray with a tray cloth in fine white lace, and when Vincent enquires whether he can take it to them she says no, that she will do so herself.

She knocks gently on their door, and she can hear the rustle of bedclothes. The door opens, and she smiles, a cheery good morning on her lips. Penelope is there, and there is not a stitch of clothing to her. Leila very nearly drops the tray. She averts her eyes and hands in the tray and pulls the door shut, and not very gently either in her consternation.

She quickly goes out to the veranda for a breath of fresh air. It is chilly, and as she flops into one of the cane chairs, she pulls the light quilted wrap that she is wearing tightly around her. It takes a minute for her to get her breath back. And she is glad. Glad that Penelope is surely a blonde. A genuine one. And glad that it was she, not Vincent, who had carried the tray in to them.

GRASS IS GREEN, THE SKY IS BLUE

He better, Malati tells herself, *he better do well.* Look at all the effort she has put in, three months of painstaking planning three months of time and energy expended, three months of making sure that everything was just right. And it all depends on today, on those five or ten or fifteen minutes. And what if it doesn't go well? What then is she going to do? Ravi is of no help whatsoever, with his office, his job, his travelling on work, his tensions, his having to work on weekends, and the endless phone calls even when he is at home. *Single-handedly*, she tells herself, *I've done all of this on my own. Thank God he has at least condescended to put in an appearance today, taken two hours off from his precious work. Look at him, all curled up under his quilt, sleeping like an overgrown baby, with a day's growth of stubble on his cheeks and under his chin. How can he? Isn't he even concerned? We've got to be there in three hours' time, and here he is, sleeping soundly as if he hasn't a care in the world. Never mind*, she tells herself, *let me deal with Tarun first. I'll get to Ravi later.*

She runs through the stuff in her mind as she hurries through her morning ablutions. He seems to know most of it; yes he does. But knowing is one thing, saying it all and correctly is another. He's so moody. That is what worries her. Can't blame it on lack of practice, of that she is sure, for the sessions have been many and relentless.

'What do you say when you go in?'

'Good morning, Auntie.'

'What is the colour of the sky?'

'Blue.'

'What is the colour of grass?'

'Green.'

'Spell *rat*.'

'Aar-aa-tee.'

'What comes after four?'

'Six . . . no, five.'

He gets his arithmetic mixed up all the time. That's what she ought to focus the practice on this morning. There's the possibility of a full half hour between now and departure time. She better bathe him and change him once again into the same pyjamas that he is wearing. Changing him into clothes specially procured for the occasion this early is dangerous, for Tarun has a natural affinity for dirt just as dirt, it seems, has a natural affinity for him. And this combination of affinities can be pretty deadly, as she has learnt from continuing experience, for her new Whirlpool is no match for the streaks of yellow and brown and grey that get smeared evenly back and front, making her often wonder how he manages to at points of the anatomy that normally one requests another to scratch or, sometimes, would use a longish pencil for, or the pointed corner of a plastic ruler. But he manages to, and with aplomb, which is why she is going to change him only minutes before departure, for the clothes he will wear are pristine clean and specially bought for the occasion. A pullover in pale shades of blue and cream to set off the dark blue of his jeans and the sparkling white of his Bata Adidas, all of four hundred just for the shoes, but Malati is sure the investment is justified for an event so momentous, so critical to their lives, and is worth every paisa spent, only she hopes it is all worth it and things work out well in the end.

Mrs Trehan seemed confident all right yesterday during the last-minute confabulations, and she said he was ready, said she'd spent the last three months ironing out every wrinkle, and she knows what kind of testing they do and what nature of questions are asked and she feels he's been thorough. 'That's why Prep Time is so popular,' she said. 'That's why we are in such demand, it has a cent per cent placement rate, and you can indicate your choice of schools, one and two, and we focus, we prioritize, we prepare the child in that order. The trick lies as much in mastering technique as in knowing what each school wants. Like Progressive gives top marks to diction and correctness in spoken English, St Mark's to scores on the test paper, Gyan Vikas seems pleased with a good memory. The nuances are what are important. And then there are some newfangled ones that don't test the children at all or at least claim not to—no pressure, they say, they merely interview the parents, and they promise no homework, and they promise that the child will be happy.' But Mrs

Trehan says she doesn't trust them one bit, for what with Mandal and all, 95 per cent is the bare minimum for a decent college. 'Let us wait and see,' she said. 'All this rubbish about all-round development is okay, but let us see how they fare when it comes to the crunch.' *As if interviewing the parents alone is going to do any good,* says Malati to herself. I mean, Ravi and she can talk their way through, she is sure; give them all the answers that they want to hear, or even worse, like she heard the other day, about this chap who had a not-so-smart spouse and he took along his sis-in-law, his younger brother's wife, who is convent-educated and all and communicates well. How could the school ever find out that they weren't man and wife? Or that mischievous friend of theirs, Nishant, who told the folks on the interview board that he wakes up every Sunday and spends a half hour with his son and tells him the story of the *Mahabarat* episode that comes on TV at nine and they watch it together. The board was awfully impressed, whereas she knows for certain he doesn't surface any Sunday until ten, and most often nursing the nastiest of hangovers. So much for these new varieties.

It is half past six now, and it is two and a half hours to departure, and Malati wonders whether she should wake Ravi up but decides no, he will only come in the way of last-minute preparations. She walks across to Tarun's bedroom, and he is deep in slumber, lying diagonally across the bed, his right hand folded under his head, his head resting on the crook of his elbow, having discarded his pillow sometime during the night, the quilt off him and crumpled at the foot of the bed, knees slightly bent, a hint of a smile stretching his lips ever so slightly, dreaming maybe some quiet little dream of his very own of patting mud pies into shape, of rolling in sandpits, or of climbing on to the bonnet of their dust-laden Maruti or maybe of licking jam off fingers grey-brown with dust and grime. Malati shakes him gently, and he lets out a tiny whimper as he opens his eyes, reaches down the bed, grabs his quilt, and attempts to snuggle under it.

'No, no, Tarun,' she says softly. 'It's time to wake up.'

She lifts him off the bed, cuddles him on her shoulders, his face close to hers, and whispers in his ear, 'Wake up, you've got your interview today, remember?'

It had been quite a struggle getting him into bed early the night before, and Ravi had been surprised to find him fast asleep when he had got home at eight. Eleven hours, that's what he had needed, and that's what he had got. Malati is pleased. At least he won't be grouchy on that count. She carries him into the bathroom where his toothbrush is at the ready, a small blot of toothpaste on the bristles. He stands on tiptoe and leans into the washbasin to brush his teeth and to gargle, and as soon as he finishes, he is installed on the throne. He is a bit wider awake now, and she asks, 'What will you say when you go into the room?'

'Good morning, Auntie.'

'What's the number of your car?'

'DBC 3686.'

'What is your telephone number?'

'6486346.'

'Very good, Tarun. That's very clever. And what will you say if the auntie gives you sweets?'

Thank you, Auntie".'

Progressive liked polite children, or so she had been told.

'What colour is the sky?'

'Green . . . no, blue.'

'What colour is your sweater?'

'But, Mama, I'm wearing pyjamas.'

That brings her back to the present. Soon he is scrubbed and clean, and Malati and he are on the bed reviewing, first, the alphabet. And then the numbers.

'What comes after three?'

'Four.'

'After six?'

'Five.'

'No, seven, Tarun. Seven.'

'Seven,' he says.

'Understood?'

He nods his head gravely. And so it goes on, a full half hour more. And then it is time to haul Ravi out of bed, and he grumbles. She nearly loses her temper and tells him, 'Don't you have any sense of responsibility? Look at me last month with you away in Bombay. I was up at three, and I left Tarun with Lakshmi at home, and it was freezing cold standing outside the school gates, but at least I was somewhere near the head of the queue, and I got the registration forms, which I believe a lot of ones that arrived at earthly hours didn't. You ought to be ashamed of yourself, he's your son after all, do you want him to study in some so-called convent school like St Anne's around the corner that has nothing Christian about it? I know it is owned by a Mr Kohli. This is the one chance, let me make that clear, because getting into any other higher class in any worthwhile school later is impossible, so better take today seriously. And I am told that the crowds there are huge and you often have to wait, which is why is told you to take the first half off, not just two hours, so don't keep looking at your watch and grumbling, it's your son's life after all.'

She makes sure that all of them are ready and breakfasted at quarter to nine. Ravi has on a neat blazer and grey flannels and a pale-blue shirt with a deep maroon tie, and she is in a subdued deep-blue silk, not a very expensive one and not striking in the least because she doesn't want to be in any manner conspicuous. It's only a ten-minute drive to the school, but she insists on going early so that Tarun gets used to the setting, the atmosphere. Ravi grumbles under his breath but doesn't dare go further, and wisely so, because he has judged the tension in the air nicely and knows that the smallest spark can end up in a conflagration. And so they are at the school at five to nine, and there are lots of parents like them there already, and Malati gives him one of those I-told-you-so looks out of the corner of her eyes. And they sit side by side, Tarun between them clutching her arm and taking in the atmosphere. Malati feels Ravi could do with some coaching too.

'You've got to tell them that you spend time with Tarun in case they ask. I know you don't, but they like parents who do. So you've got to, okay? And don't talk a lot.

Crisp, short answers. I believe that's what goes. They don't much like the garrulous, show-offy varieties. And please don't pick up any arguments even if you disagree with something that is said. That is absolutely the wrong thing to do. And don't cross your legs when you sit. And don't slouch in your chair.'

'And you must say "Good morning, Auntie" when you go in,' says Ravi.

Her eyes bristle with righteous anger.

'Don't you take anything seriously?' she asks him. 'Your son's life, his most important day until now, and this is how you behave!'

'Sorry, sorry, sorry,' Ravi says. 'I was just joking.'

'This is no time or place for jokes.'

And soon it is half past nine. A list of names are read out—ten of them, Ravi counts—all given appointments at the same time as them, and they are number 6 in serial order. That means even at ten minutes for the test and ten for the interview, it's two hours at the very minimum. But he doesn't grumble or peep at his watch, merely fidgets around on the hard wooden bench on which he is seated.

And the children are called in turn and are led in like so many lambs to the slaughter, wide-eyed and nervous, and mothers walk a part of the distance and whisper final instructions in their ears. One stubbornly refuses to go, and the mother carries him all the way to the door of the room where the testing is to take place. He starts bawling loudly, and that prompts yet another to start in chorus. The result is that all the mothers start looking slightly wild-eyed and curse the howler under their breaths, praying that their offspring don't behave similarly. But the pleas for divine intervention are of no avail as a couple more join the chorus. And one petite young lady in a designer suit and a pashmina, who you wouldn't think would hurt a fly, administers a sharp one on the rear side of her ward sitting next to them, and his bawling only increases in pitch and intensity. The next moment, you hear a loud stage whisper as she pleads with him, 'Please don't, Abheek, please, please, please, for my sake please, if you love me.' And she is alone, the father either at work or a late sleeper, or maybe she is a single parent in the manner of the day. Tarun is stoic through this melee and gets up and goes without demur when his name is called, and you can see the pride in Malati's eyes as she clutches at Ravi's arm in relief. Tarun is back fifteen minutes later, looking none the worse for wear. Malati asks him, 'What did they ask you to do?' and he says 'Everything.' She asks, 'Did you know everything that they asked?' and he replies in the affirmative. 'Numbers?' He nods his head. 'ABCD?' He nods his head again. 'Jigsaws?' One more nod. He can do fifty-piece ones with consummate ease; that's the extent of practice. 'Did you do everything correctly?' A nod again. Malati seems satisfied. She is more relaxed now, and she actually smiles at Ravi and tells him, 'Now it is only the interview that's left. I'm sure he will do well.'

And suddenly she's nervous again and asks Tarun, 'What will you say when you go into the room?'

'Good morning, Auntie.'

More waiting. Tarun wants a go at the swings, the slide, and the jungle gym that he sees in the distance.

'Please, Mama, please,' he says.

'No, no,' Malati tells him, 'you can't. You will get your clothes dirty.'

Another half hour passes, and Tarun fidgets constantly. One more appeal to proceed swingwards is turned down. And then, finally, it is their turn. Malati gets up, brushes a speck of something off Tarun's sweater, gives Ravi a once-over, and leads the way purposefully, the other two following a couple of paces behind. They open the door on which a brass plate reads PRINCIPAL and go in. There is this rather tired-looking old man well past middle age sitting behind a table of intimidating size, who looks up and gives them a wan smile, a smile from which he can't work out the boredom, for this is the fifth successive day of interviewing, and there are well over two hundred under his belt already. Tarun smiles at him as he has been taught to and says, 'Good morning, Auntie.'

The man looks preoccupied. Maybe he hasn't heard, Malati hopes.

'Not *Auntie, Uncle*,' hisses Malati in Tarun's ear.

Ravi stifles a sudden urge to giggle.

'Good morning, good morning,' the man says.

Relief is writ on Malati's face. He's missed the *auntie* bit.

'Sit down, sit down.'

They sit, Malati perched on the edge of the chair, Ravi straight-backed and with uncrossed legs. Tarun looks a little bemused but by no means overawed.

'What is your name?'

'Tarun Shankar.'

'How old are you?'

'Four.'

'What does your father do?'

'He works in the office.'

'What does he do in the office?'

'He eats lunch. Mama sends him big tiffin every day.'

Malati is squirming in her chair, helpless.

'What is your phone number?'

'6486346.'

'What are the colours on your sweater?'

The sweater is made up of two large squares. He points at each in turn.

'Blue. Yellow. See, Mama, it isn't even dirty.'

Tarun turns to the principal.

'She told me not to get it dirty, or else the auntie will get angry.' He pauses for a second as realization dawns. 'But you are an uncle, not an auntie. Where is the auntie?'

Malati looks as if she wants to crawl under the oversized table and die. The little squirt. All that effort, all those rehearsals, and now this.

'Why? Don't you like me?'

'No,' says Tarun. 'You're ugly.'

Malati has this insane desire to get up and run. Even Ravi's throat is drying up. Tarun is oblivious, and his eyes scan the room as he sits on the chair, swinging his legs, a beatific smile on his face.

'Mr Ravi Shankar.' He looks at Ravi. 'Where do you work?'

Ravi tells him.

'Is the job transferable?'

'Yes,' says Ravi. But it is unlikely that he would get moved out.

'Thank you,' says the principal.

'B-but is that all?' asks Malati.

They stand up and file out of the room, and it is silence all the way to the car. They drive off, and you can cut that silence with a knife as they approach the last traffic light before the stretch to their house. The light turns red, and Ravi slows the car to a halt. And the dam breaches.

'It's entirely your fault,' Malati tells him, her shoulders heaving as she sobs into the *pallu* of her sari.

'If only you would spend more time with him, he wouldn't be like this.'

Ravi is silent, wisely. Tarun edges up from the rear, puts his head forward between the two front seats, looks bemusedly at his mother, and pipes up, 'But, Papa, why is Mummy crying?'

* * *

STAR QUALITY

*H*is name spelt magic at school. I remember vividly the first time I heard it said. It was a Sunday afternoon, and I was scurrying towards the loo next to the common room. I must have been around twelve at the time, on the threshold of adulthood yet childlike in my innocence. The birds and the bees, I mean. Excepting for snatches of half truths that I had picked up en route. I knew that babies didn't arrive stork-borne. I knew that a man and a woman had to marry for progeny to emerge. Yes, being married was an absolute must. Beyond this smattering, very little.

A thin, pimply faced, fair-skinned boy of around fifteen was hovering around the bathroom door, and he put a hand out to stop me as I tried to rush past.

'But I want to have a pee,' I said.

I am sure you remember how it is that age. Hold on till the last critical moment, till your bladder is about to burst, oblivious to the need until the pressure is almost at breaking point.

'No, you can't go in there.'

'But I want to have a pee,' I repeated, rather balefully.

'No, you can't. Not here. Go upstairs, will you? Don't you know Geoffrey is having a shag?'

'Who's Geoffrey?' I asked my friend Raju when I got back to the common room later. The radio was blaring Hindi songs, a few boys were managing to read amidst the din, a gang of four was playing a noisy game of carom, and two others were huddled over a chessboard. A few were lounging around, just killing time. The decibel level was high, and added to that was the radio at full pitch, trying to drown the rest of the voices.

'Geoffrey Gordon, don't you know?' His tone showed surprise.

'Who is he?'

'Oh, I forgot. You're new here.'

Just then, the individual who had stopped me at the bathroom door entered, followed by a tall, good-looking boy. He wore a T-shirt and trousers, and his hair was combed neatly back, not a strand out of place. He had a broad chest, a slim waist, and strong legs. His clothes fitted him tight, and the contours of his body rippled with taut muscle as he ambled in.

'That's Geoffrey,' whispered Raju, his tone reflecting a mixture of admiration and awe.

Almost like saying Clark Gable. When I look back, the star quality was unmistakable. The easy, elegant gait, the direct stare from large brown eyes neatly spaced. The aquiline nose, the firm, square chin, the broad forehead. His skin was a pale golden brown, peculiar to the gene mixture of the Indian and the Anglo-Saxon races, burnished satin smooth by the tropical sun. He stopped somewhere near the centre of the room and looked around, as if expecting obeisance from the occupants. And yes, all action did indeed stop; all play was suspended. As he glanced around, he spotted me.

'New here, are you?'

'Yes,' I said. 'I am.'

'He's been here just a week,' piped in Raju, eager to please.

'Where you from?'

'Kerala.'

'Beautiful place,' said Geoffrey. 'Lovely girls. Remember Nalini, Jim? One of the best.'

'Yes, Geoffrey, one of the best,' said pimply face.

'You got any sisters here in school, man?'

'No,' I said. 'I have only a brother. And he's too small to even come here.'

'Too bad, too bad. Hey, chaps,' he addressed the trio near the radio, 'how about some decent music? Cut out that native crap. Try Australia, will you?'

My first encounter. Geoffrey Gordon was numero uno all the way. Or almost all the way, I guess, because he had flunked once already, which is why over the next five years, I saw a lot of him. He passed out just a year ahead of me. He wasn't the academic sort, but so what? He was everything else. Everything. School colours in soccer and hockey. Sang with an attractive, full-throated voice. Ran a strong hundred meters. Moved so well when he danced, his natural agility bolstered by a grace and flow that had a strange primordial quality. The twist was nothing for him. The shake was when he really took off, when the girls couldn't take their eyes off him. All the varieties. The aaps and the natives. The Marjories and the Lindas, the Patricias and the Violets, the Malinis and the Ushas. All gazed at him unabashedly, a mixture of wonder and devotion, that quality of something badly wanted yet out of reach, out of reach but not quite, if only they tried hard enough. No wonder they clustered around him, especially the others. The natives had to be more discreet for proximity would have meant all manner of trouble if the folks at home got to know. But gazing from a distance was permitted. And over the years, from adolescence to near full manhood, Geoffrey had assimilated all this adulation, assimilated it so well that it was a part of his being, reflecting in all that he said and did. Things came easy to him, and he knew that they did. Mother Nature had taken care of that well enough. And the arrogance that this endowed him with was not the sort that you could dislike, for it came to him so instinctively, so naturally, a wholesome sort of arrogance that reflected in the light bounce in his gait, in the manner in which he held his head, in the directness of his gaze, in the charm of his smile.

Yes, we all worshipped him in a way, I included, knowing all the while, deep within, that I never could be one like him, for I wasn't made that way either physically or in the mind. An ordinary bloke, if you get what I mean. Better than the average at studies, an all-rounder of the moderate variety. Not a bad-looking chap but hardly striking—at that age all arms and legs, gangly. I didn't excel at any sport, but I wasn't exactly bad either. House team, yes, but no school colours. Run of the mill, without seeming self-deprecatory. Nothing like Geoffrey. He had it all. Not unintelligent, either. His flunking was more attributable to the numerous distractions that were a part of his daily milicu than to any serious lack of intellect, for he was quick-witted, ever ready with the fast repartee.

And it was during that one month each year, in January, that Geoffrey really came in to his own. The sports events, half a dozen cultural competitions, the Annual Day. And Geoffrey was there in every one of them, not just present but dominating the scene in his own inimitable way. I can't say how far his exploits with the girls took him for this was the season when continued proximity was not merely permitted but an essential for things to function smoothly. Rumours abounded, grew fast into legends that only added to his already larger than life image. Yes, we were all envious. Who wouldn't be? Of his gumption, his looks, his flair, his style. But we gave him his due and tried hard enough to emulate him, often resulting in stinging slaps that left ears ringing. One of us would succeed may be once in a while, a hasty stolen kiss in a dark corner of the green room, and that meant a straight ticket to heaven. Geoffrey went much further than that, or so we heard. But who knows? He was a discreet sort, and never were there any witnesses. Geoffrey it was, Geoffrey all the way. Or so they said. And his acolytes grew in number, a half-dozen acne-ridden varieties that waited on him, worshipped—or so it seemed—the very ground he walked on.

* * *

I can feel the train slowing down to a halt as I come awake. It has been a well-deserved holiday—relaxed, indolent, large quantities of fresh fish and gallons of beer. I feel slightly guilty. The extra weight will need working out. I draw the curtains and peer out. It's Basin Bridge, ten minutes at best to Madras Central. My wife and my four-year-old are soundly asleep, snuggled under blankets, for the air-conditioning had been turned on high at night. I prod them awake, ring for the attendant, give him a tenner for services rendered. He helps me pull out our suitcases and sundry stuff from under the berth, arranged in a line for the porter who would be on board even as the train slows down. Five minutes later, the train glides into the huge asbestos-roofed shed that houses the railway platforms. A porter appears at the door to our unit, clad in khaki shirt, a dhoti, and a red turban.

Less luggage, more comfort, or so the ancient Indian Railways adage goes. My wife isn't a believer. Three large suitcases and an assortment of cartons tied down with multicoloured nylon string. We need a trolley, which means waiting on the platform. I fidget, impatient as ever. The trolley arrives, and we start off, I just behind the porter, my wife and son a couple of paces further back.

Our initial passage is quick because most of the crowd near our train has already departed while we were waiting for the trolley. As we get closer to the main exit, the crowds thicken again. The trolley is useful in clearing the path for us as our porter yells, 'Give way!' I am directly behind him, and I urge my wife to catch up since all three tickets are with me, to be handed over to the ticket collector at the exit gate. I have always wondered how effective this system is, because at peak hours, the traffic is so great that a lone man hasn't an earthly chance of doing an effective job of the collecting. The Railways has its own wisdom and ways, I guess.

It is rarely, if ever, that I notice the person at the gate. No one does, I am sure—just shove your tickets into the outstretched hand and jostle your way through. Yet another soul in a slightly soiled shirt, crumpled black jacket and stringy tie, nondescript, possibly bored to death with the tedium of his job. It's just that Arun, my son, jostled by someone, stumbles as we approach the gate, and I bend to pick him up, right opposite the spot where the man stands. And in stooping down to scoop him up, I glimpse the man's face. And start walking down, past the exit, about half a dozen paces or so, and stop. And stand there, Arun in my arms, my wife a pace or two ahead following the trolley, oblivious to the fact that my progress has been arrested. And turn around and look at the chap at the gate once again, this time a little more carefully, my eye more discerning.

Geoffrey. Are you sure? Yes, no doubt about it. But not the same Geoffrey. A receding hairline, listless hair plastered to his scalp with sweat. Puffed-up cheeks and a nose grown grotesquely bulbous. A waistline that stretches open the last button of his shirt just above the belt. And a bored expression on his face. Not sullen, just bored. Forlorn. An expression that seems to convey a lack of meaning in what he is doing, perhaps in life itself. I continue to stare. Through the movements of the crowd, he catches my eye and I, his. I try a half smile, but there is no response, not even a faint hint of recognition on his face, as his eyes shift focus to someone in front of him. Maybe he does recognize me, for I haven't changed substantially in face. Maybe he actually doesn't. Maybe he doesn't want to. I walk on to catch up with my wife, who by now, having noticed that I am not at her side, is looking around her as she hurries to keep pace with the porter and the trolley.

* * *

SLAM DUNK

*I*t is only a little past half past six and it is dark already. The setting October sun is an unnaturally large orb, coloured a strange deep red, so dimmed is it that you can look at it directly and not hurt your eyes, its rays softened on their way down through the many layers of smoke and dust that lie suspended from the sky above like veils of grey gossamer. Amar leaps off the DTC bus as it slows down and sprints alongside it before coming to a smooth, unhurried halt. That is the smart thing to do, not wait until the vehicle has reached its appointed stop. And he is strong and fit and agile, which is why he is able to alight with such ease, such grace, not losing his balance even one bit. His own physical progress has never ceased to amaze him. Look how puny he was, all sticklike arms and knobby legs even two years back when he was in the eighth—who could have ever guessed then that he would grow to be this way—the heavy school bag strapped across his back, no load to speak of despite being overstuffed with books, loaded to bursting because it is a weekend and there is a lot to plough through. An inch or two more upwards and his height would be ideal, and then he would be a permanent fixture on the team, he is sure. His shooting skills are already good; he can down three pointers at practice, one in two with ease. His shoulder muscles are taut with the weight of the bag about them, and he feels a surge of self-assurance. No more does anyone attempt to bully him as some of his nastier classmates were wont to do in the not-too-distant past, not anymore, they wouldn't dare, not with those rippling pectorals. As he turns and walks down the path that leads to where he lives, Amar smiles to himself. *Very little to grumble about*, he tells himself.

He passes the apartment downstairs as he approaches the stairwell that leads to where he stays on the first floor and the neighbours' TV is on, a filmi program of some sort, he can hear music and he can hear a clutter of voices too, Sanjeev and Sumitra and their mother. He is half tempted to step in and spend some time, get offered tea and pakoras maybe, and converse a little, but no, he reminds himself, there is so much to get through. It is just three weeks to the half-yearlies, and as Papa often reminds him, 'Sports is good for you, yes, but remember the rat race is deadly too. Eighty per cent and above is the bare minimum even for a half decent college, let me tell you, there is no escape from working really hard.' Amar nods to himself gravely as he climbs the grey-brown cement stairs and stands outside to insert his key into the night latch, for it is dark and the single uncovered forty-watt bulb that shines in the landing isn't really adequate to see well by.

As the lock unlatches, he leans his shoulders against the door and pushes it open. He enters the apartment and places his bag full of books on the dining table. It is a two-room set, a living room and a bedroom with an attached bath. He turns the light on in the bedroom, and there are two beds within, close to each other, leaving enough space between them and the wall for him to do push-ups on the cold grey stone floor. Which is what he does without bothering to climb out of his school uniform, just takes his shoes off, fifty at an even pace, making sure that he holds his body up each time till his forearms ache. And a hundred sit-ups follow, leaving the muscles in his calves and thighs trembling. A light sweat is all that this produces. Soon after, he returns to the living room, opens his school bag, and searches within for his chemistry text, for he has a test Monday, sulphur and sulphur compounds. He better mug the equations up wholesale, he tells himself; he doesn't seem to be able ever to balance them correctly.

Placing his book on the table and his bag underneath, he walks into the kitchen, and turning on the light within, he reaches down to the wooden plank beneath the slab on which the gas stove rests and extricates a frying pan. It is one of the non-stick varieties, its black Teflon insides showing streaks of dull silver where the ladle has scratched in the process of stirring. The subziand the dal are in two lookalike steel vessels, each covered with a flat round steel plate, stored there since morning when his father had finished the cooking before rushing off to work. Won't spoil, really, the weather is cold enough. All he has to do is to warm them up and pour them back into the same containers and keep them covered. Papa would be back in fifteen minutes at best, and he likes to eat as soon as he comes in, right after he gets through with making the rotis. Amar would love to do that part too, save Papa the trouble, but his attempts haven't been overly successful. They seem to come out shapeless, amoebalike, and they don't roast consistently either. Amar pours a spoonful of oil into the saucepan before he pours in the subzi to make sure it doesn't char, and as he heats it gently, it smells good. Must say Papa has improved a lot, considering what it was like when he started off. He understands what a rush it must be finishing off all this and then going off to work so early. Amar has often offered to help, but Papa says no, so all Amar does is get his own breakfast ready, a couple of boiled eggs and three or four slices of buttered bread. Not his favourite menu for dinner, dal and a sabzi subzi, but he well knows that they can't afford a lot more with only one income coming in now. Which is why he so looks forward to the Saturday trips to the dhaba close to the main road, where he chews on chicken tikkas and piping hot rotis and laps up rich, thick dal on which the oil floats temptingly.

The heating is done in all of five minutes, and he carries the stuff to the dining table. As he puts it down, for a moment, just a moment, his mind goes back to what was, the two of them at the table, waiting for him to return from work, and as they heard his footsteps on the stairs, the sounds of the footfalls as distinctive as a person's voice, she would be in the kitchen rolling the rotis so that they would come piping hot to the table as soon as he got there after a quick wash. And Amar always opened the door for him.

A lump slowly forms in his throat, and Amar clenches his fists and tells himself, *You've got to be brave, you've been that all these past many months since she passed away, now why all this?* And he bends his elbow and feels his biceps round and hard with his other hand and tells himself, *I'll make it, I will next year to the playing six,* and he closes his eyes and there he is—he can see himself feint, sidestep, crouch, spring. And the ball glides smoothly into the basket. It only he were tall enough to slam dunk, now wouldn't that be something! And he hurries to the bathroom and keeps the basketball game going firmly in his mind, an unchanging picture frame that helps keep out any other that might attempt to intrude.

He bathes in a hurry—Papa might come in any moment— and he dries himself and comes out of the bathroom in his underwear. He stands sideways to the full-length mirror in the bedroom, pulling on his pyjamas, when he catches a glimpse of his own back in the glass, and his back glistens with tiny droplets of water where the towel hadn't reached. And he hears her say, 'Now how many times have I told you, Amar, to dry yourself properly? Look at all the water on your back. Your kurta will get wet, and you are bound to catch a cold.' And he picks the towel up from the bed where he had placed it and towels his back vigorously before he pulls his kurta on. And suddenly, there is a lump in his throat again, and he shakes his head and blinks and a tear—large, warm, salty—unfetters itself from the corner of his eye nearest the bridge of his nose and rolls gently down his cheek. He swallows a large lump that bobs his Adam's apple up and down. As he moves towards the living room, he hears his father's footsteps, and he swallows one again and blinks—no, he can't let Papa see him this way. He has promised him, hasn't he, that he would be brave. And slam dunkers don't cry anyway.

* * *

ALL THE PEOPLE
ALL OF THE TIME

*Y*ou can fool some people for some of the time, or so the adage goes. But not all the people all the time. I am not so sure. It depends on how you define the term 'all the people'. For if the people you fool are large enough in number and are fooled for a sufficient length of time, I suppose you could say that it proves that there are exceptions to the adage. I am living proof of it, I dare say.

It isn't that I had to opt for this vocation and no other, for I guess I could have been anything in life that I wanted to be. I was intelligent enough. I knew that even then. And persevering. And whatever the choice I had made, I would have excelled at it. Of that I am sure. But the conventional never did hold any fascination for me. The strange, the out of the ordinary, is what excited me always. That is why I am what I am today, I suppose.

I find it difficult today to look back in time and say with a great degree of certainty how I got induced into this trade, unusual as it is. What I can make out through the shrouded mists of memory and time will be at least part conjecture, I am sure. Yet I can single out two events, which seem somehow to stand out and hence perhaps have relevance. The first, a seer with an impossible hairdo, robed in saffron, who I saw climbing out of a Mercedes-Benz— a bottle-green one if you please—more than forty years ago when I was a mere stripling just into my teens. I don't know what impressed me the more. Maybe it was the sight of the people who flocked around him, worshipping, it seemed to me, the very ground he walked on. Or maybe it was the Merc. Either way, I do have a definite memory of being taken in by what I had seen and observed. Very much so. And an impressionable age, to boot. The other event, I have always liked to believe, is my reading the Guide, a book that held me spellbound. If Raju could accomplish all that unbidden, unwilling victim of happenstance, what couldn't I do if I contrived to make things happen? Confidence is important in this trade. No, not confidence of the confidence-trickster variety. No tongue in cheek intended, please. I mean confidence in self. Confidence in one's competence. Confidence in one's abilities to succeed.

Just as with any other trade, this one too has a specialized body of knowledge. And requires special skills. And abilities, which as I look at it, are skills in action. That is what makes a profession. That is what I am. A professional. And mind you, no retirement age, no redundancy, no fears of being superannuated. Lifetime employment, if you please. I am close to sixty now, and if all goes reasonably well, I have at least fifteen active years ahead. When I retire is of my choice. It sounds almost like a good capitalist, doesn't it, like an industrialist who has built an empire from scratch, an empire of great assets and healthy reserves, except that in this case the assets are the human beings who flock to me, the reserves their worship, their adulation, their faith in me. No, I am not going to run away with my secretary like I was told one of my younger professional brothers had recently done. And decimate with one impulsive act, what has taken me over thirty years to create and shape? Not a chance.

Taking you back to the professionalism bit. This profession requires a lot of very hard work, I can assure you. And a tremendous capacity to absorb, retain, analyze, interpret, and communicate. Much more than what other professions require, probably. And it requires gargantuan effort to start with. As bad as studying for engineering or medicine, a share worse probably.

Take me, for instance—when I started off the only Gita I knew well was the girl with rather well-developed mammaries that I was deeply enamoured with through my second year at college. How ironic, I tell myself when I look back now. Today I can send crowds into rhapsodies when I interpret the other Gita, the one that Krishna of the ebony hue composed for his Partha as they rode into battle along the dusty, blood-splattered plains of ancient Kurukshetra. Poetic lines, what? Just shows. That one possesses reserves deeper than one imagines. That the soul in the end is unfathomable. Just as the universe is. Just as God is. I should stop this here, I think. Let me not get carried away. I do enough of this regularly without my having to go on about it.

Let me take you back to the beginning. The hard work part. Five years of intense study to begin with. The Gita, the Upanishads. The Ramayana and the Mahabharata are like primers at school—compulsory reading. Even the Vedas, a quick guided tour, of course. A detailed one can take all of twenty-five years. Not enough time for that. I had a great guru, a classy guy. Sincere, dedicated. Must have been some premonition that made me opt for Sanskrit at school and college. In part, at least, it was because I was a dead loss at Hindi in any case. But I am a natural at most other languages, and that made things fairly easy for me. Yet the work was hard. Let me emphasize this: your grounding better be good, or you are bound to get caught out in the end. It's like my maths teacher used to say at school. Get your basics right, and everything comes easy. Goof up there, and even simple problems seem inordinately difficult. And let me also tell you, you've got to be in touch all the while. It's like being a doctor. Just because you acquired an MRCP twenty years back doesn't mean you can continue to treat your patients today without keeping up to date. You've got to read all the stuff that you can get hold of. I have an extensive magazine subscription list and a large, ever-growing library. You've got to know a great deal about a variety of things, and a very large variety at that. I mean you can't assume the folks still like the Beatles when what they actually dig is Dire Straits. And you just have to know what is happening at the World Cup when your congregation is full of Germans. This is what I figure fascinates them the most—this facile, effortless bridging of east and west, this seeming equal comfort with aspects of both; the material, factual of the one; the spiritual, philosophical of the other. That's why I am especially popular, I suppose. I vibe with all sorts. But let me assure you, it is backed up with a lot of very solid homework. No running away from that.

In some ways, my profession is akin to a classical vocalist's trade; in both, the voice box is critical. Imagine a guy with a squeaky soprano trying to defend Ram's latter-day treatment of Sita to a flock of a thousand. I am sure you can't. You're right. It just won't work. What you need is a rich, throaty, husky baritone. Like mine. And it need practice, needs constant toning and conditioning like anything else. I do it with the aid of a tape recorder, a sophisticated piece that has come via one of my well-endowed disciples from Germany. Keeping them spellbound is a trite way of describing what you can do with a good voice. *Mesmerize* sounds better. What you say is important, of course, but as important is the magic of your voice.

And your eyes. You can't have Mongol doing a Kathakali feature now, can you? Likewise, you can't work this trade with slitty eyes, sleepy eyes, even the slightest hint of cross eyes. Emphatically no. This isn't the movies and Norma Shearer. Never hear of her? Before your time, probably. Closer to mine. She had the sexiest squint going. But let me not wander. Your eyes. They have to be large, they have to sparkle and shine, they have to draw those folks out there looking at you deep into their hidden recesses, limpid pools of cold fire that invite them and then draw them in, into the ecstasy of your gaze. Tall order, all right, but let me tell you, in this trade, it is all important. One of the keys to success.

Let's come to build now, to physical stature. Five feet ten is the minimum I would prescribe, rather like the president's bodyguard, I suppose. You have to tower over your flock, you see. You do have the advantage of sitting most of the time on an elevated platform. But you aren't seated all the time. You have to mingle. You have to let them touch you, let them feel you, let them know that you are real, yet so different, so infinitely superior. And you can't be five foot nothing and do that. Physical fitness doesn't seem to count for much. I am reasonably trim myself, but that is out of personal choice. I know of many sloppy successes, three chins and a paunch that precedes by a good foot. Height, then, is definitely of consequence. Girth isn't. On to beard growth. Incongruous, isn't it, to talk of something like that? But important nevertheless, let me assure you. Beards are kind of part of our uniform, if you have noticed. No place here for sparse or straggly beards; thick, full foliage is essential to set off those piercing eyes. Follicular growth on the scalp isn't a must. If you bald gracefully like I have with the hairline receding at a steady, gentle pace, the broad, bare expanse of forehead and upper deck is a neat foil for the eyes and the beard. And as I have aged, the salt and pepper seems to have only added to the grace of my demeanour.

That's enough of the physical, I think. I have gone on too long already. Let us get to the softer side of things, to what's within you. What God has given you. The gift of the gab I've covered already, I think, and so also intelligence. They are absolute prerequisites. You won't get anywhere without them. But in my own experience over the last thirty-odd years, just as important, just as crucial if you want to succeed yet also enjoy yourself and retain your sanity, is the ability to laugh at yourself, to not take yourself too seriously. Else with the kind of blind, unquestioning adulation that you are bound to receive, the slippage into shades of megalomania can be easy, where you end up believing everything you say and what others say about you. And if that happens, God help you, because you are bound to lose yourself, lose your location, your moorings, your sense of direction. The spiral then can be fast and steep, and before you know it, you are a prisoner of your own fantasies. Why fantasies? You start thinking that they are real. I have been careful not to fall into this trap. Many are the chuckles I have had as I lie at night in my splendid bedroom with its silken drapes and its feather-soft mattress, the air-conditioning set to exactly seventy-eight degrees, which is my preference. I must have referred to the temperature in passing sometime, perhaps in jest. I don't recall when. See how easy it can be to lose yourself when every passing whim of yours is taken in dead earnest?

And now for the strict taboos. I'll be as brief as possible. I don't want to scare people off. Alcohol and tobacco are out. And drugs of any variety. Those are the very things that the folks that flock to you are trying to run away from. Never forget that. And, boys and girls, sorry, no sex. Not in my book, at least. No wild ecstatic orgies, no girls creeping quietly into your bed at night. I am not against women disciples. The more, the prettier, the better. They set off your masculinity, your suppressed virility. But no sex. With them or with anyone else. Absolutely not. Which is why I recommend entry into this trade like in my case at thirty or thereabouts, when you have sown all the wild oats you wanted to, when you feel you can live without for a lifetime. Though shit. I know. But that is the way it is.

I haven't put you off, have I? The stuff that makes for success in this trade are pretty tall orders. And the taboos can be intimidating when you think of them. Yet let me tell you, there is an upside too. And what an upside! That feeling of power. That feeling of being able to reach down, deep into people's souls. That feeling of being able to hold in the hollow of your hand the emotions of those hundreds that flock to you that buy your spiel. Forget the material comforts. They are there. They become of little consequence after a while. It is like the very wealthy anywhere. After a stage, money and creature comforts are of little meaning. Because you know they are there. Forever. It is then that the quest for power takes over. This is the path of all conquerors, of all builders of great empires. This is mine too. Yes, life isn't a smooth, even bed of roses. You will have your hiccups. Like some disillusioned disciple leaving you and then calling you a charlatan or a rake. Or worse. Yes, some are bound to see through you, pierce your carefully built, well-preserved façade. You have to live with that, take it in your stride. Occupational hazards, as with any means of livelihood. Let me assure you, however, that as long as the basic underpinning is there, the essential competences are present, the law of averages works. And you are there at the top of the heap, like me.

Why have I gone on and on and at such great length about all this? you may very well ask. Let me get to that. I am not getting any younger, the late afternoon of my life, so to say. Twilight approaches. The shadows lengthen. I know I am physically in pretty shape. Won't drop dead all of a sudden, at least that is what I think. But who knows? My tragedy is that I have no one to succeed me. Yes, I know. I have this group of so-called favourites who surround me always, who serve me ever so faithfully. They are all nice people. I like them all a lot. I really do, else they wouldn't be there any way. But not one of them is worthy of succeeding me. Unfortunate, but that's the way things are. Take the three prime contenders. Their Holinesses Nityananda, Chakrananda, and Shraddhananda—exotic names, what? A nice resonance to them. All of my own coinage. I chose them essentially because they sound so nice, to be frank. Take these three. The first named is intelligent and articulate, but dark, ordinary-looking, and five feet four. No way. The second one is tall and handsome with a thick full beard and piercing eyes. He is articulate on the surface, yes. His voice is good too. But his endowment of intelligence is rather meagre. That rules him out. The third has all the prerequisites in abundance. He has only one drawback—he is English. White-skinned. Sorry, but this institution is essentially Indian. Like the Church of England is English. Can you imagine a West Indian Archbishop of Canterbury? Neither can I.

I have an Englishman to head my outfit. I am very fond of John, yes I am. But in this instance, sorry. No go.

That is why I am on the lookout. I often think, half in jest, of what an ad for this would look like. Wanted: an intelligent, articulate, linguistically inclined, tall man endowed with large eyes and a good deep voice. Good beard growth essential. Should be able to laugh at himself. Preferred age twenty-five plus. Males only; sex, alcohol, drugs taboo after employment. I have been waiting for more than five years now, ever since I first thought of this. But the right man just hasn't come along. I don't know when he will, if at all. And if he doesn't, then what will happen to all that I have built up? I can't let a lifetime's effort wither away. Time is running out for me. Slowly but inexorably. I'll keep searching, I suppose, until I come across the right chap. If not, who knows?

* * *

FULL CIRCLE

*I*t is a Sunday in early March. The mild Calcuttan winter is slipping its way relentlessly into the stifling months ahead, but it is still comfortable enough. It is a cloudless day, bright and clear, with a mild breeze blowing that wafts its way into my room, gently ruffling the thin half curtains that drape the window. The house is quiet, and I am thankful for that as I try to concentrate on the book that lies open in front of me on the table.

My exams are just a fortnight away. The very idea of their proximity gives me the jitters, for as Pa keeps telling me, it is imperative that I do well. A little sacrifice now will be more than worth its while, for my future will largely depend on how I perform. And that has meant compulsory confinement to the apartment, a kind of house arrest that I have chosen to undergo these last two weeks or so. Which is why there is no cricket game this Sunday morning. And no strolling along Park Street later in the evening with my friends, eyeing its younger female denizens hopefully. And no sneaking a beer or two shared between the four of us at the bar at the corner of College Street. And having arrived home, just about in time for dinner, no washing out the remnants of a mouthful of paan in the basin in the corridor at the rear of the dining room and hoping that my breath doesn't exude the odour of beer and keeping a safe distance between me and the rest of the folks, especially Jaya, whose olfactories are extra sensitive, the sneaky little so-and-so. I am sure Pa, if at all he gets to know, is merely going to shrug his shoulders and say to himself, 'Boys will be boys,' because I am certain Pa did all this and more in his time and he likes his tot in the evening now. But best not to take avoidable risks anyway.

Which, briefly, is why I am at my desk in my room this balmy morning, just perfect cricket weather, and I am trying hard to concentrate, and I am nervous for there is two years of syllabus to go through, and I berate myself mentally and think, if only I hadn't left everything to the very last. If only I had shown some discipline. However am I going to get through all this? I won't do well, I am sure, and then there will be hell to pay. I don't seem to be able to remember anything, anything at all, especially Eco II, which is what I am ploughing through at the moment, or trying to at least, and which used to be the last period in the afternoon twice a week, and who had the time to be in class so late each day when there were so many more important things to do, more important and more interesting? The words seem to come unstuck in my mind seconds after I read them, and I berate myself all the more for Pa isn't the interfering type, and he likes to believe that I am the responsible sort and capable of looking after myself, but I know what it is going to be like if I do badly, actually. Pa is a bit stiff upper lip and perhaps a little taciturn too—comes from being ex-army, compounded probably by his working now for this Brit outfit—and his fuse is long, but I know from experience that when he blows, the pyrotechnics can be daunting.

I attempt to pull myself together and curse Maynard Keynes and all his ilk—sod the whole lot of them—and try to concentrate once again on the notes in front of me.

But I feel thirsty just then, and I get up from my desk and walk through the door towards the fridge in the dining room. As I pour myself a glass of water, I hear Pa moving about in the living room. I can see him from where I stand, and he is all dressed to go out, lunch someplace, I suppose—chilled beer and lamb and mint sauce. Now that I like. I can't wait to finish college and get myself a job somewhere, maybe one of the tea gardens out in Assam where life is interesting and the living is enjoyable, or so I am given to believe.

The doorbell rings just then, and I wonder who it is, for we aren't expecting anybody, all entertaining having been deferred for a while so that I wouldn't be distracted. Ma and Jaya are out visiting. And folks don't normally just land up without telephoning beforehand. Pa opens the door and his 'Yes?' isn't unfriendly, but I am almost certain that it isn't someone he knows.

'May I come in for a moment, sir?'

The voice isn't familiar. Curiosity makes me step into the living room on the way back to my desk. There is a youngish man at the door, dressed in the green grey of the Indian army, lieutenant's pips on his shoulders. His uniform is neat and well pressed. The brass shines; his black shoes gleam. A few years older than me—at best, twenty-five. He is fair, with thick black hair combed back, long but not long enough to break any regulations. He has pleasant features, clean-cut, if you know what I mean.

'Please do, what can I do for you?' My father steps aside, and the visitor comes in.

'My name is Sujit Wadhwa, sir. I am a lieutenant. In the army.'

'I can see that, young man. I am an army man myself. Took premature retirement soon after the war a few years ago. What is the problem?'

'I got into Calcutta only this morning, sir. I am Mr Kohli's nephew. You probably know him. He stays on the ground floor.'

Our block of apartments is three-storied, and each floor has two large airy flats. We live on the first floor, and the Kohlis live directly below us. It is not that the Kohlis and we are close friends or anything, but Pa knows him reasonably well, for they play bridge together at the club once in a while.

'Yes, I do know Mr Kohli,' Pa replies. 'But he and the family are away on holiday, aren't they?'

'Yes, sir. That's the problem. I have my bags outside their door. I was planning to wash and change and go to the station and try and get on to the Howrah Mail in the evening. You see, I wasn't being sanctioned my leave, and then all of a sudden, my CO changed his mind. We are posted on the NEFA border, sir, so there was no way I could make any booking in advance.'

'That is no problem. You can bathe and change here, if you so wish,' said Pa.

'No, no, sir,' said the lieutenant. 'I can't impose myself on you like this.'

'It is no trouble at all,' says Pa. 'In fact, I absolutely insist.'

The lieutenant relents reluctantly. He pauses for a moment, scratches the back of his head, and gulps.

'There is something else, sir. I don't quite know how to put it. It is so embarrassing.'

'Never mind. What is it?'

Pa is solicitous. Such a pleasant young man, so well-mannered. The army still selects well. I can almost read his thoughts.

'I had my pocket picked, sir, of all things. This morning, on the way out of Howrah. Neat job. Didn't feel a thing. But you know how crowded the place is. You are constantly being jostled around. Pretty foolish of me, I suppose, letting my wallet remain in my hip pocket.'

'You won't be the last,' replies Pa with a short laugh. 'It happened to me a couple of years back. Same place. I had gone to see off my sister.'

'I had a tenner in my shirt pocket,' says the lieutenant. 'Can't for the life of me remember when or why I placed it there. Lucky though that I had. That is how I managed to take a taxi here. Sorry, sir, but that is the way it is.'

'Happens to the best of us, as I said. But don't worry, maybe I can lend you some money. You can always return it on the way back to the unit. The Kohlis will surely be back by then.'

'I am most obliged, sir,' says the lieutenant.

'How much does a ticket to Delhi cost?' Pa asks.

'A hundred rupees, sir. But that is for a first-class ticket. I can manage a seat in second. About fifty for that, maybe.'

'An officer and in second? That wouldn't look right.' Pa pulls out his wallet. 'Here, you better keep a couple of hundred extra. That will see you through comfortably. And be careful, please. Not in your hip pocket, not at Howrah at least.'

'I don't know how to thank you,' says the lieutenant.

'Maybe Jaideep can come with you to the station. You can manage that, can't you, son? He is waiting for any little reason to abandon his books. I am sure he'll be most willing.' He smiles at me. 'And have lunch before you go. I have to go out myself, but Leela—that is my wife—will be back shortly. Why don't you get your bags up from Mr Kohli's floor? Jaideep, do help him.'

And we go down together to pick up a suitcase and a weather-beaten holdall, and just as we get back, Ma and Jaya return and are introduced. I show the lieutenant the spare bedroom where he bathes and changes and emerges in a little while in a deep-green T-shirt, tan slacks, and brown suede loafers. And he is lithe and muscular, and Jaya can't take her eyes off him. He makes himself comfortable in the living room as he lounges on the single-seater, Jaya seated opposite to him to the right, eyeing him wistfully. And Pa had asked me before he left for lunch to be sure to offer him beer. He says yes, and I pour him a large pewter mug full. And as he takes it from me, he asks me if I wouldn't join him. Jaya has to pipe in just then, and thank God Ma is out of earshot in the kitchen. I am ready to strangle her, I am.

'He does,' she says, 'he does actually. But he is afraid to here, because of Ma.' She giggles.

The lieutenant refuses to be drawn into taking sides.

'Never mind,' he says. 'You will be getting a job soon, I am sure. Then you will be on your own. It is a good thing in any case not to overdo these things while you are in college. Once in a while is okay. Too often may not be advisable.'

I nod at him.

'What do you plan to do after college?' he asks.

'I am not very certain yet. My father wants me to sit for the competitive exams, but I am not sure if that is my cup of tea,' I reply.

'Ever thought of joining the army?'

'Not really.'

'It isn't a bad place to be actually. Life is a bit nomadic, but you soon get used to it. On the whole, I would say that things are quite good. Even in a remote place like NEFA. And more than anything else, the excitement can be exhilarating.' The lieutenant leans forward. 'What is the army if you haven't smelt death through your nostrils. Right? I haven't been in a war yet, but NEFA is bad enough.' He pauses. 'Just around ten days ago, for example. I was leading a patrol, and we were returning to camp, around five miles away. And they were waiting for us around the halfway mark. Daylight was fading, and so spotting them was difficult. And the first shot that was fired went whistling past the side of my head. A quarter of an inch to the right, and who knows? I may not have been here talking to the two of you. We lost two men that evening. It is a dangerous life, it is, but worth every minute of it if you have a bit of the daredevil in you. And the pay is good too. I am enjoying myself quite a lot, actually.'

He is quite the raconteur. And he is polite and pleasant too. Even Ma is bowled over. And as for Jaya, the kind of moony eyes that she is making, she won't hear the last of this from me. Not in a long time. He has a healthy appetite too, or maybe you don't get very much to eat on the slow trains that come in from the east. Anyway, the hilsa is turned over to perfection. And the curried mutton is just right. And it isn't just the lieutenant who eats well—I do too, as if to celebrate this unexpected holiday and maybe also to quell the unease that is hovering within me, a result of the inevitability of the fact that I would have to work doubly as hard to make up for lost time.

It is not long after lunch that it is time for him to go, and he does so after Ma and Jaya make him promise that he would spend time with us on the way back, perhaps join us for a meal. And he promises them that he would, and he takes leave of them at the door, and I walk down the stairs with him, carrying his suitcase for him.

When we reach the courtyard and are walking down the cemented path that leads to the gate, he looks at his watch and turns to me and says, 'You don't really have to come with me. It is nearly three in the afternoon, and I know what exams are like. Why don't you go back up and settle down to your books?'

I say no, that Pa had said that I should go, but he is persuasive, and I agree in the end, and I watch him as he turns the corner on the road past our house, lugging his suitcase and a rather scruffy holdall. And when I go back so soon, Ma and Jaya aren't pleased, and when I tell them that he had insisted, they say that I ought to have gone nevertheless—such a nice chap, so pleasant, so well-mannered.

'And so handsome,' I whisper to Jaya in an aside and get scratched on my arm with those long talons of hers. Heaven knows why she grows her nails so long; they look positively ludicrous, if you ask me.

The day passes with me confined to my room and my table. During the weeks that follow, with the high-voltage tension of the exams and with the whole family rallying around me, even Jaya, the lieutenant is forgotten. The Kohlis are back a couple of weeks later, and Pa mentions the lieutenant to Mr Kohli casually at the club one evening but elicits only a blank look. And Pa doesn't enquire any further, and neither do any of the rest of us, and there is no sign of the lieutenant on his way back east. And the subject isn't brought up after that. But as Pa says me to me the only time we talk about it, 'Such a nice young man. Must have been a misunderstanding of some sort somewhere.'

* * *

The weather is just perfect, as it is sometimes at this time of year. It is a November morning twenty-five years into time, and I am in Delhi, an Assam refugee of sorts. Pa has journeyed some time ago into the pale blue yonder, and Ma has too, a couple of years back. Jaya is married and far away, in the United States, and she doesn't seem to have changed one bit; she is as precocious as she always was, at least with me.

Ranjana, my wife, and Usha, my daughter, are out shopping. Ranjit is out playing cricket—a lovely day for a full day's game, the sun bright yet mild, the breezes gentle and soothing. I am idling through a magazine, waiting for lunchtime, sipping a glass of cold beer, uncertain about what to do with myself.

The doorbell rings. Who could it be? I wonder to myself. We aren't expecting anyone, and folks normally don't just land up before telephoning beforehand. I peer through the eye glass fixed into the door and see a man there, mid fifties, wearing an army uniform. I open the door and say 'Yes?' not in an unfriendly fashion, the kind of tone you use with someone you don't know, and the man says, 'May I come in for a moment, sir?'

Now you don't let strangers into houses in Delhi, not unless you have a strong instinct for suicide, and so I don't step aside or invite him in but stand at the door and ask him what he wants, and he says, 'My name is Sujit Wadhwa, sir, I am a major in the army.'

And I stare at him unbelieving, and the features fall into place as the frames emerge clear and true from the recesses of my memory. Lieutenant Wadhwa at the door, smiling a little doubtfully at my father, the lieutenant with a mug of beer in his hand, lounging on Ma's single-seater upholstered in deep maroon corduroy, the lieutenant as he gesticulates in the middle of a narrative emphasizing something, the lieutenant looking back and waving as he turns the street corner near our block, carrying his suitcase and his weather-beaten holdall.

And the look that I give him is strange or disconcerting or both, for he mutters an 'Excuse me' and turns and hurries down the drive. Ranjana arrives at just that moment and parks the car outside, and Usha climbs down and is opening the gate. And as Usha opens the gate, the lieutenant walks straight out, and the last I see him is as he trudges down the road in CR Park on this balmy early winter afternoon, lugging along a suitcase and a rather scruffy holdall.

THE ORACLE

*I*t is cold. Why am I here, I wonder, in the dead of night, the track that we are traversing barely visible! Moonlight filters along the edges of dark clouds, lining them a dull silver in silhouette. The path is rough, not well used. That is bound to be, for this part of the riverbank is of no use to anybody. No grass to graze on, only boulders and strewn rock. The Chambal is a rough river. Rough and wild and majestic. A ravine river. Parts of it resemble a Norwegian fjord, for the water is as deep blue and the depth countenances no end, or so it seems. The banks are tall and steep. Climbing down them is not easy, let me tell you, especially in the half-light of a cloud-filled moonlit night. And it is spooky. The wind whistles—around what I don't know, for there are no trees around. Yet it whistles and it moans. It is past midnight, rendezvous time with the oracle. A live human one, a local specimen, one, it is claimed, who can give you the answers to anything. Or so claims Jaiveer Singh. A friend's friend had told him. And Jaiveer's determination to meet this character is why I am here at this late hour, in the middle of nowhere. Why me? Cosy in my house, two large whiskies down, at peace with the world, about to tuck into some succulent koftas and wafer-thin piping-hot rotis. Why me? But I am never one to refuse. He knows that. And I am single. That matters a lot when you dream up outlandish schemes.

We had picked up a torch on the way out, but it isn't of much use. The batteries seem to be on half power, probably run out through disuse. The light that it emits is no more than a subdued amber glow on the ground, rather like the radiance from the dying embers of a fire. All around there is silence, an unreal silence broken only by the wind, a silence that echoes our shambling walk as we stumble along the rough path that leads to the river's edge.

'We are almost there,' says Jaiveer, as if to reassure me.

'Are you sure you know where we are going?' I ask. 'There doesn't seem to the anything around for miles.'

'Of course I do,' he replies. 'Just be a little patient. We are almost there.'

I am no sure-footed mountain goat. And I suffer from keen vertigo. The climb down the riverbank is as bad as going down a cliff, or so it seems to me in the near darkness. I ask Jaiveer to slow down, and he does so reluctantly. *I am not getting into any improbable schemes of this sort again*, I tell myself. It is different coming for a night shoot properly equipped with powerful flashlights and hip flasks of whisky to keep you warm. This is different, and I am not terribly enthused. After what seems an interminable journey down, we are on flat ground once again. But there is nothing around as far as I can see. I express my concern.

'Hey, are you sure this is the right place?'

'Of course I am,' says Jaiveer. 'Can't you see there, beyond that dark rock?'

It is a couple of hundred yards away, partially hidden by a large boulder past whose dark outline a faint glow shows. As we approach the spot, I can make things out a little clearer. A small bonfire, made from twigs and logs washed ashore during the monsoon, parts of trees that line the cliffs some thirty miles upstream, dried to easy inflammability by long days in the soft winter sun. There are two of them around the fire. One is an old man wrapped in a coarse blanket, folds of a dhoti showing in patches from underneath. He has an extremely wrinkled face and a seemingly lean, almost emaciated frame. His companion is much younger, looks to be around thirty years of age. He is clad in white pyjamas and a kurta buttoned up to the throat. An old, thick coat of rough wool covers the lot, two sizes too large for him, reaching well down his thighs.

'Is this the oracle?' I ask Jaiveer.

'Yes. Keep quiet,' he admonishes. My amusement must have penetrated even the still darkness around for Jaiveer whispers, 'There is no need to snigger.'

We approach the fire and sit down on the side of it opposite this incongruous couple, cross-legged on the ground. The earth is hard, stony, and cold. My jeans are thick, but it is still uncomfortable. The old man doesn't acknowledge Jaiveer's greeting in the local dialect, but his companion does. We sit around, waiting. The river water, across which a soft wind blows, has the effect of an air conditioner. In winter. I am chilled to the bone. It is almost as if the old man isn't looking at us, is staring straight through us. He is absolutely still, an unlikely sculpture that has found its way as if by mistake to this strange, lonely spot. He closes his eyes, and it seems to me that he is getting to be even more still than he was before, almost rigid. The stiffening continues for all of five minutes, and I wonder, *What next?* And all at once he starts to tremble, from head to toe, every part of him. The trembling increases in intensity until it is almost as if he is shaking. The blanket slips off his shoulders, and his gnarled, reed-thin body is before us, clad only in a cotton dhoti. Doesn't he feel the cold? I glance at Jaiveer, but he is oblivious to me, his eyes intent on the eerie quivering figure before us. In the half-light of the low fire, the shadows slip and slide across his body as the shaking reaches its violent climax.

His companion pipes up suddenly in the local dialect, 'Victory to the Goddess!'

'Victory to the Goddess,' repeats Jaiveer.

I don't say anything. My diction in the local lingo is imperfect, I know, and I don't want to cause any offence.

And then the oracle speaks, in a soft, quavering voice that rustles like a gentle draught into the silence around us. I can barely understand what he is saying, but Jaiveer later told me it went something like this. 'I know you. I knew you would come tonight. I have been waiting for you . . .'

He describes who Jaiveer is and traces his lineage five generations backwards. He extols the virtues of Jaiveer's family, which has ruled part of the land around for many centuries. All the while the companion sits, palms folded in a namaste in obeisance to the Goddess who speaks from within. And yes, he knows why Jaiveer has come to him. The family has fallen on hard times—relatively speaking, I suppose—for from what I had seen they lived extremely comfortable, if indolent, lives. He can help. He knows the answer. There is gold. Not a lot of it but enough. Within the precincts of Jaiveer's dwelling. 'It is buried,' he says, 'near the well behind the house.

'Listen to my directions carefully, for I will say them only once. Walk thirty steps from the well, directly east. Then ten steps north. And then five steps west. Dig at that spot, and you will find it. In a wooden box.'

The oracle falls silent. Suddenly, a few seconds later, he begins to shake violently, almost where he left off the first time around before he started to speak. The shaking subsides into a tremble and the tremble into the strange stillness that had enveloped his body when we first saw him. It is another five minutes before the old man opens his eyes again and stares right through us, or so it seems, into the blue-black void beyond, seeing things that ordinary eyes such as ours cannot perhaps see. He looks exhausted, as if having undergone enormous physical stress. The sweat glistens on his brow and on his shoulders, sparkling ever so slightly in the dying firelight.

Jaiveer gets up. I follow suit. He moves towards the companion and bends low, placing some money on the ground beside him. The companion doesn't glance at the money; he merely folds his palms together in farewell. We trudge our way back to my motorcycle, and I can sense Jaiveer's excitement, though he doesn't say anything. It is really cold on the ride back, even colder than on the way up, cold enough to invite Jaiveer in to warm himself up with a drink. He is reluctant; seems to be in a hurry to get home.

'Don't be funny,' I tell him. 'You aren't going to start digging at this hour in the morning, are you?'

When we are inside and seated, a drink each in hand, I ask him about the old man's monologue. Jaiveer narrates. My scepticism is probably evident on my face.

'Come on, don't tell me you believe in all this baloney. He must surely have known beforehand that you were coming. And anyone around knows of your family. Nothing startling about that. And the gold—that must be what most people hereabouts must be coming to him for anyway.'

'He isn't from here,' says Jaiveer. 'His village is almost sixty miles away.'

'As if that is the other end of the world! Come off it, Jaiveer, don't tell me you take all of this seriously. I can't understand you guys sometimes. A part of all of you seems still to be in the fifteenth century. Oracle, my foot. Good way of earning easy money, I suppose. Requires practice, yes. The shaking and the trembling, I mean. I am sure the old man and his help must be pissed drunk on local brew by now.'

Jaiveer doesn't seem to be in a mood to carry on with the argument.

'Forget it,' he says. 'You probably won't understand.'

'When are you going to dig for this pot of gold at the end of the rainbow?' My sarcasm is overt.

'Tomorrow. You can come over and join me if you feel like it.'

'I think I will,' I tell him. 'After spending half the night getting my arse frozen in the cold and my knuckles and knees bruised clambering up and down cliffs, you bet

I'll be there. To watch you dig a hole right through to China. You've got the directions right, haven't you? If you excavate half the backyard, your mother isn't going to like it very much.'

Jaiveer swallows the last of his drink.

'See you around five in the evening tomorrow,' he tells me brusquely, as he gets up to depart.

It is close to two when I sleep. The next day is a Sunday. Thank God, else I would have nodded my way through the day. I have to work, you see, unlike these friends of mine, to whom life is one endless bout of shooting and drinking and eating. And lots of sleeping, of course. Can't do without a siesta in the afternoon. Lucky sods.

* * *

I am there on time at five the next evening, curious despite my scepticism. It is twilight, the winter sun almost at the horizon. The wheat fields behind Jaiveer's house, past his backyard, glow a rich orange red. Jaiveer has already measured the paces, and a shovel and a pickaxe are at the ready, covering the spot. He does the measuring once again for my sake. Thirty steps east, ten steps north. He pauses and looks at me. Five steps west. Jaiveer picks up the shovel, starts digging. We are out of sight of the house.

No one can see us, thank God. *Two imbeciles*, I tell myself. Jaiveer has been digging for over ten minutes now, the hole a foot square, a foot deep. When will he grow up? I ask myself. It is all of twenty minutes now, and the hole is two feet deep. My cynicism seems vindicated. The digging continues. The earth is dry and hard and doesn't yield easily. Jaiveer is tiring.

'Want me to take over?' I ask him.

'No,' he says. 'I'll manage.'

I can't believe this. That I am here, digging for treasure, gold that an unlikely charlatan in a so-called trance has said is here. It is all so unreal. Maybe *comical* describes it better. It is another ten minutes, another six inches at best. The progress is getting slower. I feel like repeating my 'hole through to China' line, but I don't have the heart to. Jaiveer looks so forlorn.

'Isn't that enough?' I ask him.

He doesn't answer but continues to dig. *I might as well enjoy the sunset*, I tell myself. I gaze at the wheat stalks rippling gently as a soft breeze blows across them, their colour a shade redder than their natural hue as the sun completes its last paces for the day. The only noise around is of the twittering of birds as they wing their way back to the trees around the backyard where they nest and of the swishing grate of Jaiveer's shovel in the soil. I take in the tranquillity, the quiet, soft beauty of the pastoral setting.

That is when I hear it. The thud of metal on wood. There is Jaiveer strengthening up, the sweat staining his T-shirt, his jacket on the ground beside him, a look of exultant triumph on his face. And I, looking positively incredulous, I am sure. A veritable tableau, the wheat fields and setting sun behind us a fitting backdrop. A tableau that bridges the centuries. And I wonder.

* * *

CATCH

I am wearing a white shirt starched and pressed to unnatural stiffness. My trousers of grey flannel are spotlessly clean, the creases sharp to a fault. My tie is striped deep red and grey. My shoes are laced up neatly, the assiduous application of polish and elbow grease showing up gleaming as it should. The collar of my shirt is a shade tight and cutting into the skin around my neck. My hair is Brylcreemed and brushed carefully back off my forehead, along the upper reaches of which a thin film of sweat has started to show. I carry a natty leather folder, which is placed on my lap as I sit, legs straight so that the creases of my trousers remain intact. My fingers drum lightly across the folder. The chair on which I have been placed is large, overstuffed and intimidating, and the upholstery seems to surround me, to smother me, adding to my natural discomfort. There is only one other person in the room sitting across me at a table on the far side, youngish, comely, yet somehow forbidding in appearance, or so it seems to me, as she rifles through a sheaf of papers staked in front of her on her desk. She is seemingly oblivious of my presence, as if she has consigned me out of her immediate consciousness after having brusquely told me to wait, that Mr Meadowes is not free, not just yet. I squirm a little in my chair and drum some more on my folder, not audibly of course, for the silence in the room is of a strangely penetrating variety. It is as if I am afraid that the slightest movement from me would be construed an act of desecration, except of course the rustle of paper as Mrs Williams leafs through the stack in front of her, but that sound seems only to complement the silence. And so, probably, would the clack of her shiny deep-green Remington that rests on an extension of her table on her right as she sits facing me.

I have this rather sudden urge to cough, or at least to clear my throat, but I suppress it and say to myself, *Don't*, and I try to hold on, but I can't because the back of my throat itches so, and in the end, I manage a half cough, half gurgle and am rewarded with a sidelong glance that speaks of irritation and a countenance that seems to say, *These types, trust them not to know even how to clear their throats gracefully.* I squirm a little more, and the speed with which my fingers move noiselessly across the folder doubles.

Balls, she's anything else but Indian, I tell myself in an attempt to make myself feel better. Not even one quarter of her, I am sure, all dressed up in a skirt and a blouse and bobbed hair and pretending to herself and the world that back home is Trafalgar Square and the Thames, and I am sure the furthest she has been is the soda fountain at Elphinstone or—maybe I should be more charitable— Flury's on Park Street when she went to Calcutta visiting cousins. All an assiduously cultivated put-on, these airs and graces, as when I came in fifteen minutes ago and she spoke in a carefully clipped accent that belies the engine driver types that she used to cavort around at the Railway

Club not ten years ago. That feels better, yes it does, and the intensity of my drumming decreases, and I pick up the gumption to cross my legs, carefully, so as not to disturb the creases. She's back to her papers, back to pretending that I don't exist.

'Excuse me.' I'm myself surprised at this sudden display of valour, probably the resultant of a combination of anxiety and boredom. 'Would it take much longer?'

She raises her left eyebrow. It requires talent to do that. Or it's got to be there in your genes. Or maybe relentless practice can help. I've tried often enough but haven't quite mastered the trick. Both always go up together, else the best I can manage is one slightly up and my nose all puckered to one side. Practice in her case, I suppose, not genes. I console myself.

'I told you already, didn't I? Mr Meadowes is busy.' Now what exactly is that supposed to mean? 'Is it going to take much longer?' is what I had asked. I already know that Mr Meadowes is busy. Snooty bitch. But I swallow my pride in a great gulp that rolls my Adam's apple around my throat.

A bell sounds from inside, a soft tinkle that floats past the closed mahogany door with its polished brass knob. Mrs Williams pushes her chair back, gets up, and glides past me as she opens the door, closes it as gently as she opens it, and disappears from view. It's as if I have suddenly gained freedom, and I indulge myself in the luxury of clearing my throat, stretching my legs, and mopping my brow all at the same time, as if to complete all of it soonest, as if each one would have fetched its own separate reprimand of the one raised eyebrow had she been in her chair. My rather unseemly haste isn't necessary, it seems, because it is another ten minutes before she reappears and, qqpretending that I don't exist, occupies her chair once again. And it is another five minutes before the soft tinkle is heard again from inside and she deigns to raise her head, look through me, nod in the general direction of my chair, and tell me, 'You may go in now, Mr Meadowes is free.'

I stand up, straighten my tie, shoot my cuffs, and stride in confidently and purposefully, or as near that as I can make do, in my attempt to shush the butterflies that have started to flutter in my stomach.

'Good afternoon. Sit down, please. Mr Menon?'

'Yes, sir.'

The office is roomy and furnished in simple yet elegant taste. Mr Meadowes sits behind a large well-polished teak table on a chair upholstered in deep maroon leather. There are three similar upholstered chairs, smaller but of like design opposite to him. At the far corner on the right is a neat arrangement of sofas, a low centre table in the middle. It is obvious that Mr Meadowes is a wildlife enthusiast, for the numerous prints on the walls are devoted to that subject. The cool January air in Coimbatore permits the windows to be opened and the drapes to be drawn.

Mr Meadowes has a large, full face, thick eyebrows, and small, very blue eyes. Though his face is fleshy and probably a testimony to good living, his body isn't flabby at all from what I can see, which is good going for someone who looks to be in his late forties.

'Where are you from?'

'Calicut, sir. In Kerala.'

'Schooled there, did you?'

'Yes, sir.'

'And college?'

'Madras, sir. Christian college.'

'Economics, I see.' He has been looking through the typewritten two-pager that contains my particulars. 'And now you want to become a planter. Any particular reason?'

'A friend of mine joined your company a year ago. Achutan. I met him the other day, and he seemed to be enjoying what he was doing, which is why I decided to try.'

'Enjoyment, yes. But it means very hard work too. During the season, you may have to put in twelve-hour days for weeks at a stretch. Are you capable of that? And life can be lonely. There can be times when you won't see anyone but your men for days on end. Will you be able to take that?'

'I think so, sir. I haven't done this kind of thing before. I'll try my best, nevertheless.'

All at once, Mr Meadowes begins to look distracted, and his manner turns a shade brusque.

'I'm not sure we have any vacancies now.' My heart falls. 'We'll get in touch with you if something comes up.'

As if remembering suddenly that he ought to be polite, he gives me a half smile. I stand up. Just then, the door behind me opens, and Mrs Williams peeps in.

'Sorry to bother you, Mr Meadowes, but Mr Robertson wants to see you for a moment. He says it's urgent.'

A youngish individual of medium height walks in, dressed in tan slacks, white shirt, and a deep-red tie.

'Yes, Jim, what's it?' Mr Meadowes looks up.

I am not sure if I have been dismissed. I rise but keep standing.

'Tomorrow's game, sir. We are one short. George has gone down with a fever.'

'Too bad. What do we do now?'

He is about to consign the papers containing my particulars into his OUT tray when something catches his eye. He peers closely at page 2. He addresses me.

'You play cricket, do you, young man?'

'Yes, sir. I used to play for the college.'

'What are you?'

'An all-rounder of sorts, sir. Three down bat and leg spin.'

'Good. Good. You can substitute for Smith tomorrow.' I am not given a choice. 'Got your whites with you?'

'I can manage the shirt, sir.'

'We'll lend you the trousers. Eight sharp in the morning. At the Club.'

The Planters. Achutan had told me all about it. The highlight of visits to the head office. Liveried bearers and gins and tonics in the afternoons, whiskies and sodas and lamb and mint sauce at night. Rattan on the veranda, chintz-covered sofas in the lounge.

'I'll be there, sir.'

* * *

And so here I am at half past eight the next morning on the playing eleven of Morrison and Co. The ceremonies of the toss have been completed, and Mr Meadowes, having won, has put the opposing team in to bat. I've gleaned some information in the meantime. Mr Meadowes used to be a medium-pacer of some repute in his prime, I am given to understand, having played for Sussex one whole season in the late twenties. Now, more than twenty years later, he has thickened around the midriff a bit, but his beefy arms and broad chest seem to bear witness to many a good bowl in the years past. And his action as he limbers up is smooth and graceful still. It is a bit of a grudge match, I believe, for Simpson and Stewart had won the last time around, and easily too, by over sixty-odd runs in this one—innings—each match played over a whole day. And their opening bat, John Grimmet, had whacked a fast seventy, Mr Meadowes the main sufferer. Grimmet was a mean bat and had a fifteen-year advantage in age, but Mr Meadowes still simmered.

It is a matting wicket, the rough coir a bright-green simulant turf, blending in with the grass on the rest of the ground. Meadowes goes about setting his field. I expect to be at extra cover or maybe third man since most of the rest of the team are into or approaching middle age and can't be expected to be very fast on their feet. But no, he signals me to second slip. Two slips, a gully, a point. Mr Meadowes does still fancy his bowling skills! The batsmen walk in. Grimmet is to face. He takes his guard from the umpire, marks the line with a piece of chalk picked up from behind the stumps, leans down to adjust his pads, goes down the pitch to flick away some object, maybe a pebble off the mat, returns and stands near the wicket and looks around, gauging the setting. His stance is good, bat and pad close to each other, shoulders in perfect alignment to the pitch.

I watch from second slip as Mr Meadowes measures his paces, ten short ones at which he puts a white marker and ten longer ones further beyond. My borrowed trousers are an inch too long for me and have been folded up at the bottom, but the boots fit just right. My getting a job seems unlikely, I tell myself, might as well enjoy myself. I am looking forward to the cold beer that I am sure will be served at lunch. Achutan had a lot to say about the lifestyle, which is what made me try, I imagine. Well-kept bungalows with manicured lawns, butlers, and bearers and such like, lively evenings at the club with good tennis and quiet games of billiards, whiskies and sodas, and tales swapped at the fireside, the nearest thing to ole' Blighty without actually being there. 'Good fun,' Achutan had said. But it looks like it is not to be. Mr Meadowes wasn't even lukewarm about the possibility yesterday.

First ball. Leg and middle, very little movement. Grimmet is forward, straight bat, classical action. Along the pitch, back to the bowler. Mr Meadowes bends down, picks up the ball, and walks to the end of his bowling run. He turns and charges in, face purposeful, a shade ferocious, concentrating hard. On the off stump this time, slightly overpitched. Grimmet uses the pace of the ball as he takes it at the half volley, middles it neatly as he glides it between point and cover to the boundary. Mr Meadowes's face tells all. He is visibly annoyed, and he mutters to himself on his way back. He rubs the ball vigorously down his right thigh as he walks along, and as he turns, his face has a now-or-never look about it. He tears down the grass towards the wicket at a pace that seems to say that he is putting his all into this one. Down it comes, perfect length, just outside the line of the off stump, and as Grimmet goes on the back foot and prepares to cut him square past point, the ball moves in the air that bare quarter of an inch off the straight line, a perfect late outswinger. The ball nicks the bat's outer edge and whizzes at what looks a hundred miles an hour—towards me.

Now I don't field at slip—ever. And I don't claim to have very superior reflexes. And this, for that instant, is cricket at the professional level—the bowler, the batsman, the late outswinger, the attempted square cut that gets converted into a fish outside the off stump, the speed at which the ball has come in, the speed at which it has left the bat, the speed at which it is coming at me. It is coming in at midriff level, aligned perfectly along the region of my navel. My reflexes for self-defence work, and my cupped palms cover my stomach as the ball barely scrapes them and travels with a resounding *thump* into my midriff. And I reel from the sudden pain and shock and sway, clutch at my stomach in agony, and find myself holding the ball instead. As I sink down to my knees in bewilderment, I see Mr Meadowes leaping and turning simultaneously halfway down the pitch, one arm raised exultantly in the air.

'Howzzat!' he yells.

And the umpire's finger goes up.

Mr Meadowes comes running to me, slaps me on the back, and says, 'Splendid work, young man. That was good catching. Exactly what we need at Morrison's. Great work.'

And he grins at me and turns and grins at the world as he watches Grimmet's back on its way to the pavilion. And I stroke my stomach gently and wonder if it is bruised or not.

* * *

THE BURIAL

The pit is ready, four by four by four feet, a neatly completed job, the bottom and the sides level and firm. The night is dark, only dim starlight that you can barely see by. Dug as it is in the space between a hedge and the commencement of a vegetable patch, portions of the property normally not traversed, there is no imminent danger of anyone falling in. It had been completed in the evening, and it had taken two of the malis a full hour to dig and prepare it. The sahib had inspected it personally and nodded, satisfied.

The party is about to start. It is half past nine, normal commencement time for an event for which the invitation said eight. No dress specified, yet the night is pleasant, and as the guests file in, it is mostly dark lounge suits and resplendent silk saris to set off thick chokers of pearl and glittering diamonds. The odd blazer and grey flannels is there too, accompanied by a well-tailored pantsuit, light polo-neck sweater, and Gucci shoes.

The host is a man of large build, a full face, and a strong jawline, well-cut suit, and assiduously shined shoes. A powerful person, apparently, for many of the invitees are ever so slightly obsequious, as if honoured to have been invited, and when he is greeting this variety, his posture turns straighter of back and shoulder, a shade of the imperious about it. With others there is much hugging and vigorous shaking of hands. The language of greeting varies from Hindustani to English to chaste Punjabi, depending on who the person is. The large spread of lawn fills up soon enough, and the hosts leave the entrance to mingle, greet, and converse, the stragglers who turn up even later having to search them out to say their hellos.

'Singapore is no place to shop anymore, yaar. Everything has become so expensive. And it is such a boring place. I mean, for how long can anyone survive on just good food and drink as entertainment? I can't stand it for more than three days at a stretch. I run for my life from there after that.'

'Dubai is aexcellent. Real place to go. Especially, yaar, the shopping festival. You know. Baali shoes for two hundred yooessdee. Two I bought last time.'

The tables are covered with cloth, which is white and silky satiny, the overhang in front a deep maroony red. A giant arrangement of red and white roses is placed in the centre, smaller vases placed throughout at spaced intervals.

'Oh, hellojee. So long time since I have met you. Where have you been, hiding or something?'

'I was in New Yorkjee. Kiran was delivering. A healthy baby buoy. And a citizenjee, from day one only. He can contest even for president's post, you know.'

Seekh kebabs, grilled to mouth-watering succulence. *Shammis*, the meat so finely ground that they melt on the tongue. Paneer pakodas, deep-fried, the oil drip mopped gently away with paper napkins. Salted cashew nuts, lightly roasted and still warm from the fire. *Kalmi* kebabs, *kastoori* kebabs. Thinly sliced lamb, part of a whole leg roasted over a spit fire in the true tradition of Dera Ismail Khan from whence the host, a toddler then all of six years of age, had followed his father to the refugee settlement near Kingsway Camp.

'Butjee, nothing like in Las Vegas. Prakash, you know how made he is. Lost three thousand dollars in one nightjee. I could not do anything. You don't mind a thousand rupees chaal at Diwali time, he asked me. If you don't, then this is okay also. It is aextremely dangerous place, I am tell you, this Las Vegas.'

'I know it, my Mohinder is not different. We go to Mauratious for nice holidays, the beaches are so fine, the send is like silk, and he has to play every evening. He only knows how much he lost, I don't keep countjee.'

The bearers are resplendent in white uniforms, diagonal red sashes, and turbans of red and white, while gloves with which they delicately cart around trays with glasses and eats. The whiskey is Blue Label, the gin Gordon's. The Bloody Marys are delicious, and so are the White Ladys. The evening progresses. Empty stomachs, a full eight hours since lunch. Heady stuff. The laughter gets increasingly raucous, the jokes that much bolder.

'What did the Punjabi gentleman say to the prostitute?' the raconteur asks.

Expectant silence. 'Whorejee, kigala

The garden is landscaped, surrounded on all four sides by a thick, neatly trimmed hedge along the whole length of which twinkling lights shine. The pathways that zigzag through the centre are made of smooth, polished sandstone so even that each slab seems to have been chosen individually. The lighting is soft and subdued, the glow sufficient to recognize and converse, the spacing of the lights just right, the warm yellow luminescence from the lamps setting off the rich, deep green of the perfectly groomed lawn. And up a gentle, grassy slope is the house itself, softly lit so as to set out its contours, a floor of smooth, flawless Italian marble, sofas of gentle design covered in off-white silk, drapes of like material now drawn to either side, a horsey Hussain displayed on the wall that directly faces the wide-open French windows, low coffee tables with gleaming crystal vases, arrangements of bright flowers that set off the gleaming whiteness of the ambience.

'It has been a good yearjee,' the host addresses the four or five gentlemen standing around him. 'It is a question of being able to pardict karrektly. Urth colours I saidjee, browns and greens, I was right. I sold and sold. So much that I could not cope with the demand. Jurmany, jee, and France. It cannot happen aevary year like this, but sometimes the luck is with you.' The audience nods approvingly.

Dinner is being heated up, round dishes of shiny German silver, not the flat, rectangular stainless steel variety that you would often see at weddings, and the covers have a lifting knob of polished brass. And on the side, the grill is still in operation, the kebabs having given way to tender legs of chicken, tandoori marinated to just the right succulence. The rest of the spread makes a daunting culinary array, genuine stuff, not the Pandara Park variety. Butter chicken, *palak* gosht, fish in the Amritsari style laced with coriander, *mutter* mushroom and *mutter* paneer, a jeera aloo, and a dry bhindi. Yellow and deep brown dals, their consistency just right. And a gargantuan, artistic arrangement of salad. None of the dishes float in oil, no such vulgarity. Mr Shawnee is too much of a sophisticate for such stuff. And some of the guests who have drunk in moderation tuck in the pangs of hunger rumbling in their stomachs at this late hour. Others who have imbibed incessantly find this standing and eating, fork in one hand, plate and starched napkin in the other to be beyond their capabilities of motor coordination in their current state, and in any case, the liquor has stilled their gastric juices to an extent where they are not particularly hungry anyway. The steadier amongst the eaters are the womenfolk, having consumed alcohol in small quantities or not at all. The breads are hot off the fire, an interesting melange, tandoori, nan, chaste, missy. There are piranhas too for those who prefer that, but no puris; Mrs Sawhney feels they are too oily and too messy.

It is still winter in Delhi, a late November evening, but at this hour, the night air is turning a shade nippy, a little uncomfortable despite the strategically placed coal-fired sigris. With the clock considerably past the watching hour, the party ends rather abruptly after dinner, no post prandials, much hugging and smacking of lips in the air close to Estee Laudered cheeks as the people start to exit. A half hour or so later, the last of them have departed, and Mrs Sawhney, ragged at the edges at the end of an exhausting day, a day of making sure that everything was just so, has retired bedroom wards. The caterers are packing up too, shouting to each other over the clang of utensils.

Mr Sawhney leads the procession. Two malis, two house servants. Each pair carries between them, the items for interment, large quantities, two aluminium containers full, and the loads are heavy, and it makes them struggle, stumble at times over the uneven ground. Mr Sawhney is never one to underprovide at his parties; better some waste than to suddenly find the table bereft of, say, the delectable *achar* gosht, consumed in large unplanned-for quantities. It had happened in front of him a couple of weeks back at a friend's place. Sorry, but we have run out of the stuff. Murmured embarrassed apologies. No, none of that for Mr Sawhney.

And as the entourage reaches the designated spot, thankfully, a half-moon is shining, enough light to go by, since this portion of garden is largely unlit. 'Careful,' says Mr Sawhney, 'careful,' as the pouring starts. And each container is emptied, in turn, into the dark depths of the pit made ready in the afternoon and an exotic medley of mouth-watering smells hits the nostrils of pourers. The displaced mud, stacked neatly on either side of the pit, is poured back into cover the hole; any leftover earth is spread neatly on the empty ground around. And as Mr Sawhney walks back, he nods to himself, satisfied. No, no point distributing the stuff amongst the retinue as many do; it will only end up spoiling them, create uncalled-for cravings upon taste buds used to a dal and a sabzi, and doesn't Mrs Sawhney provide them with as many rotis at each meal as they would like to eat? She isn't one of those to act measly, who rations out the stuff; she believes they work much better with their bellies full.

As Mr Sawhney enters the house, he rubs his shoes vigorously on the mat outside so as to remove any remnants of the mud and dust collected on the journey burial-wards and back. Mrs Sawhney is a dragon for cleanliness, and the carpet inside the French windows through which he enters is indeed pristine clean.

* * *

OF DUCKS AND GEESE

A midwinter bird shoot is an experience in itself for both soul and body. The best time to get at them is at first light, for that is when they lazily flap their wings from where they roost for the night in the middle of a lake or a slow-flowing river and amble their way through the air towards the fields. The early-bird-and-worm principle. Which is why, for the physical part of one's being, it is a true awakening. When the target locale is about an hour's ride away and when one has to take position by the lake side well before sunrise, it means crawling out of bed at four or thereabouts. You have a half hour with you for your morning ablutions and a cup of strong, hot coffee. The coffee doesn't just help wake you up. Its intake seems essential especially when the mode of conveyance is a motorcycle, for during the journey, the head wind seems to make a habit of sneaking its way in through whatever warm cladding you have on, and you invariably end up cursing it and yourself for embarking on such an expedition. Quite an exercise in willpower, which is why you have got really enjoy this sort of thing in order to be able to do it.

For the soul, it is an experience I often feel, in atavism. The sounds, the sights, and the smells of the jungle at daybreak as the first soft rays of the winter sun filter down to the cold, damp earth through layers of early morning mist seem to trigger off certain primordial instincts that hark back to some hoary ancestor stalking game millennia ago. The ancient savage within, papered over by centuries of so-called civilization, surfaces in a subdued and not unfriendly fashion as one adapts each time as if by the instincts of forgotten generations to the ambience around, of the waking jungle at dawn.

The atavism apart, I sometimes wonder at the pleasure that I seem to derive from such jaunts, for I am essentially from staunch vegetarian stock. Not that I am one too. Nothing like a roast goose for dinner, greylag preferably, one that has flown all way from the Siberian steppes to our table. It is at times like this that I marvel at the phenomenon of bird migration and, more than that, am thankful that it occurs. Thankful for both the shooting and the eating. But let me clarify. I am not much of a shot myself. I go along for the experience, and of course, I am wholehearted about partaking of the fare afterwards.

It was an incongruous group, the foursome that set out early that wintry morning. Two true-blooded Rajputs, father and son, a Bengali and a Malayali. Shades of national integration. In the heartland of what was once the Rajputana of yore. In the kingdom of Kotah, the *h* dropped of late has robbed the name of much of its romance and its grandeur. Abhijeet the Bengali with a newly acquired gun license, had been diligently taking potshots at tin cans outside on our large courtyard for many days. The clink of pellet on tin had improved from one in six to one in three on the average over the days. Cartridges were expensive and hard to come by, but

Abhijeet had both the spare cash and the resources. His gun wasn't a very good one, we were told, but it made do. It had been two weeks of persevering practice, and now he was ready for the real thing. Shooting flying game was different from aiming at tin cans. I think he knew that.

Gopal Singh, the leader of this group of four, was the quintessential Rajput. Short in nature, squat in appearance, and not very good-looking, he yet had an infectious smile that more than made up for the externals. He was a sort of father figure to all of us novice shikaris, and a tough and demanding teacher. His unfailing test of our resolve and, more than that, our physical resilience, was to invite us casually for a daytime shoot in midsummer when, as he used to say, the hares are lean, fast, and make superb eating. At forty-four Celsius in the shade, the test takes its toll and more. I ought to know. Tongue parched, the top of my head feeling as if the brain inside was boiling, the ground hot and unyielding even through thick-soled shoes. At the end of the day, when all of us looked like we had been lost in the desert without food or water for a week, Gopal Singh would be as untired as ever and as charming, ready for a lazy evening swilling chilled beer and swapping stories on the large veranda that ran around the front of his farmhouse. And yes, the hares made superb eating. Always even-tempered, it was amazing that in all the time that I had known him, I had never experienced him lose his cool. The loudest I had heard his voice raised was when reprimanding one of the half-dozen or so dogs that inhabited his dwelling, angry at some canine misdemeanour.

A good Rajput, as anyone would tell you, grows up to the sound of gunfire—of the cannons and muskets of war in the old days, but of late more of buckshot fired out of a double-barrelled gun, spraying pellets into and around birds passing around. And shikar to them is like football is to the average Bengali or Malayali. The months from November through March focus on this activity, and the latest flight of geese, spotted at sunset, veering towards this or that lake in the vicinity, causes as much excitement and expectation as an impending East Bengal–Bagan soccer encounter. And the way the gun butt rests light and sure on the shoulder and the way you barely see it kick as the weapon is fired surely requires as much skill as a swerving dribble into the D. My Bengali friend's skills with the gun and accuracy in marksmanship from what little I had seen would compare favourably with how the average Rajput would play soccer, more often than not lacking the subtle finesse and the comprehension of the nuances that get you on target.

The ride from town to our destination was all of thirty kilometres. It was still a dark way as we proceeded at an even, gentle pace. Shivraj Singh didn't believe in living life in a hurry. Besides, his scooter couldn't go much faster for it was a weather-beaten vehicle ten summers old that had seen many such early mornings. The first half of the journey took just half an hour. The last ten kilometres, when we turned off the regular road, involved traversing an ancient, well-used, deep-rutted cattle track where the path was so worn as to have become a gentle concave. Balancing the motorcycle along its contours was almost like riding a continuous shallow well of death. The bike constantly swung lightly from side to side, and in the darkness, with Abhijeet on the pillion behind me clutching at his precious new gun for dear life, staying upright was quite a task. The pace was slow, and at times,

I had to place my foot down as we negotiated a corner, covering my boots and half my trouser leg with a spray of grey-brown dust ground fine over the years by feet, hooves, and cartwheels.

As we rode along, the first grey-blue streaks of the half-light of early dawn fell on green squares of wheat interspersed with wide patches of bright-yellow mustard. The trees were a variety: peepal, mimosa, gulmohar, also the occasional mango grove. The large grey-black buffaloes that almost always shared one's path along these country tracks, lumbering on in an uncomprehending herd that even on a motorcycle was often difficult to drive through, were yet to venture out. So were the young children who, later in the day, would either peep from behind hedges or trees, or if we stopped, would cluster around, looking at us through large eyes accentuated by the gauntness of their faces. One of the bolder ones would often dart forward, stroke the motorcycle, and flit away for fear of being reprimanded.

A kilometre or so away from our destination, the track ended. We parked our vehicles under a large tree, loaded the three guns that we had brought along with us, and with their safety catches on, started our walk towards the river. There was barely enough light for us to see where we were going. We trusted in Shiraj Singh's usually unerring instinct for direction as he took us along a narrow track. There was hardly any grass underfoot and no sign of cultivation, for agriculture had slowly given way to wilderness. The scrub jungle around us, dry by day, glistened with early morning dew.

It is at this hour betwixt night and day, when the jungle is yet to stir, when the earliest bird is yet to venture out, when even the crickets are soundless, that one experiences the true quality of silence. An all-pervading silence where even the rustle of our shoes along the path seems somehow desecratory. When even a whispered word seems a profanity. When the stillness has a quality of eternity that transcends the humdrum of living. A silence that gives solace even as a memory.

The Kalisindh, though not as quite as forbidding as its sister, the Chambal, is, like the latter, a ravine river. Over millions of years it has cut deep through the land, forming a maze of ravines, some shallow, some deep, that traditionally have provided excellent cover for the dacoit gangs that roam the countryside a hundred miles further downriver. It was a good ten minutes before we reached the edge of the ridge and looked down at the river some fifty feet below. The sun was yet to show itself above the horizon. The timing, Gopal Singh said, was perfect. The river waters, grey in the half-light, flowed smooth and calm, just ideal for a large flight of water birds to roost upon. We walked quietly along the cliff edge, and sure enough, just two hundred yards upstream was a sizeable flock of geese floating serenely on the water.

'Greylag,' whispered Shivraj Singh, who was standing next to me. The banks of the river were bare of vegetation, of even shrubbery. We had no cover at all as a result, and going down to the bank anywhere near the flock would have meant getting spotted within seconds. Geese are very alert birds. Maybe they realize how delectable they are as food, and generations of being hunted relentlessly makes them extra cautious. The situation was tricky. That was when Gopal Singh's years of experience at this sort of thing asserted itself. It was just as a seasoned cricket captain would position a square leg here and a point there, an extra cover already in place to hold to any uppish drives. His son Siddarth he instructed to go further upriver, beyond the flock of birds on the water. We would be positioned a hundred yards further downstream from where we stood, well out of seeing, hearing, and sensing range of the flock. Siddarth would climb down to the riverbank in as much stealth as possible, move as close as he could to the birds without being observed, and empty both barrels in the general direction of the flock. The birds would instinctively fly downstream, away from the noise of the gunshot, right over us. We could well bring down six fat ones, considering that Abhijeet and Shivraj Singh had two barrels and four rounds between them. All this was said in something akin to a stage whisper. Siddharth caught on quickly and moved away, melting into the early morning mist that was now starting to rise from the river. We went a hundred yards further downstream and made our way gingerly down the steep embankment towards the riverbank. Gopal Singh admonished us, finger on his lips, indicating not a sound, please. He signalled to Anupam to move twenty yards or so further upstream. We remained where we were, and the two of us, Gopal Singh and I, sat comfortably on conveniently placed slabs of flat rock, waiting for the gunshot in the distance.

'You can smoke if you want to,' he whispered. 'It is going to take time for Siddhu to reach there.'

He didn't smoke himself. I was glad he sympathized with my addiction. I lit up and took a long drag as we spoke to each other in low tones.

'I hope Abhijeet shoots well,' he whispered.

'I can't say for sure,' I replied. 'He has been practising hard. I suppose it shouldn't be very difficult. He doesn't have to aim at a single moving target. He's got to shoot into the flock.'

'The first geese of the season,' said Shivraj Singh. 'Let's have a party tonight. Have you ever tasted my stuffed roast goose? No? Well, I can assure that you will enjoy it.'

I looked towards Abhijeet. He was glancing at us every now and then, seemingly restless. He was a fidgety person in any case. Even if Anupam shot wide, it doesn't matter, I told myself. I was thinking in the context of a roast goose for the table that evening. Gopal Singh was bound to bring down at least a couple. I thought I could sense a gleam in his eyes as he thought of the evening's dinner. To get back, saddlebags loaded with six fat ones was a great way to start the season, six fat ones that had fed well on the wheat fields for more than a month, the flesh rippling under the cover of feather. Not that the help at his farm would experience much joy at the sight of us trooping in, for cleaning these birds was strenuous work. But better than two chinks, a blue bull, a dozen rabbits, and a wild boar, which would have been an average bag fifty years ago. In the olden days, distribution to sundry relatives and friends was the norm. Today a spacious deep freeze took care of that problem.

It was about ten minutes later that Shivraj Singh tensed. He motioned me to keep still. I extinguished my cigarette and squatted crouching beside the jutting of rock on which we had been sitting. Abhijeet, who was looking our way, was alerted with a brief wave of the arm.

'Any moment now,' Shivraj Singh told me.

Less than a minute from then came the sound of Siddharth's gun in the distance. The huge flight took off from the water in a flutter of wings. For a few moments, the birds went helter-skelter until after gaining a reasonable height, they went into formation. As Shivraj Singh had predicted, they started to fly downstream, right our way.

Shivraj Singh was at the ready, crouched into firing position. His gun was on his shoulder and his eyes squinted along the barrel, ready to spring up in time and shoot, all in one fluid motion. I glanced at Abhijeet. He was half up already, weapon in hand, looking upwards. The birds formed a neat V. They would be over us in ten seconds at best, and they hadn't spotted us. The evening's roast goose seemed more real.

Suddenly, the sound of gunfire. I saw Abhijeet standing up, his gun emitting smoke. He had fired both barrels prematurely before the birds were actually on top of us. A noisy flutter of wings, and the flock veered away from us and flew out over the far bank. The lead bird came straight over us—perhaps its momentum was too much for it to control itself. I looked closely at it as it flew overhead. No wonder it seemed smaller than the rest. A duck, leading a flight of geese. How peculiar.

How do I end this tale? With Shivraj Singh's well-controlled anger—or almost well-controlled, except for one short outburst before Abhijeet got within earshot, the only time I had heard him utter a profanity? Or with Abhijeet's misery—misery that showed in the hangdog expression that he went around with for the next couple of days. Or with my own embarrassment—for though I wasn't technically a party to what had transpired, I somehow still felt a sense of responsibility. No, perhaps the best way is to describe the superb mutton curry that we had at —Gopal Singh's place that night, after many whiskies under the belt. It was spiced just right, the mutton well cooked and succulent. 'Why the mutton curry?' you may ask. Because it is an insult in those parts, a matter of untold shame, to actually buy meat from the butcher during the season, when the lakes and rivers teem with birds. The crack shots don't, for sure. But the evening was enjoyable and the curry, delicious.

* * *

THE TIMES OF INDIA, BOMBAY EDITION

*I*t was the outfit's New Year bash, organized on the terrace of the bungalow that doubled up as a private club of sorts. The do was as usual, with a lot of drinking supplemented and fortified with an array of tasty barbecued stuff. Chicken tikka, mutton *seekh* kebab, paneer tikka. And deep dried, fried vegetable pakoras, fattening and cholesterol friendly but very tasty all the same. A shamiana had been put on the terrace, the faded green, red, and other stripes looking subdued, even dignified, in the dim lighting within. Tall coal burners of a variety peculiar to Delhi's tent houses were placed at strategic points to provide warmth, for the weather around that time for year could be rather cold. The coal simmering in the sigris, together with the whisky inside him, seemed to provide Ashok more than adequate protection. A thoroughbred Bombayite, he was still only getting used to the changing seasons in Delhi, a phenomena that continued to cause him wonderment. Sometimes, things seemed so unreal, like now, when the extreme cold of late December made summer seem like a distant, unpleasant mirage. He didn't mind winter, but summer was bad; the scorching, searing heat when temperatures in the mid forties made an afternoon visit to a dealer on his motorbike pure, unadulterated hell. In December and January, he couldn't believe that Delhi could be hot in May and June, so hot that he could probably fry eggs sunny side up in his helmet after rice in the midday sun. Ashok spent the summer yearning for winter, and he spent the winter months with a queasy feeling in the stomach each time he thought of the oven-hot dusty dry days ahead.

The party had slowly started picking up pace with people coming in intermittently, some in groups of three and four sharing a car, some alone, some married couples; not everyone came for this, of course. Many Delhiites had their own bashes to get to. Getting together with old friends was infinitely more preferable to seeking the same old faces that one saw in the office each day.

The only positive point was that at least on this day, shop talk didn't take precedence. A colleague had been thoughtful enough to have invited Ashok to the party at his house that night, but he had wriggled out, knowing that except for him, everyone would know every else, and he would probably end up feeling awkward and out of place. This party would be relatively staid; a couple of senior guys were sure to land up and quench any tendency to wildness, yet to Ashok it was definitely more preferable.

The numbers had increased now, lots of natty three-piece suits interspersed with loose cardigans, baggy trousers, and sports shoes cleaned up for the occasion. A hum of conversation filled the air. The barman was busy; so were the waiters disturbing the endless supplies of eats. There was music at low volume in the background, but the dance floor or the space so designated at one corner of the shamiana was unoccupied as yet. Ashok had a colleague who was quite a raconteur, and with two large ones down, he was in his element with the group of four or five guys around him. Ashok included, in splits at some of his newer ones. That was when Ashok noticed her. Not that he hadn't seen her before. He had passed her along one or the other corridor at the office more than once, often bestowing on her a faint smile of recognition. That was a different kind.

She had looked particularly charming that night. Rashmi was no ravishing beauty, yet she was very attractive in a quite sort of way. She was petite, and she was tastefully dressed. And she was graceful, quiet, and well mannered with an intelligent face, gentle features, a jawline that spoke of determination, soft back hair cut into a shoulder length bob. She was dressed in an indigo sari, the colour of the night sky in summer and draped in an elegant grey pashmina to ward off the cold. Ashok caught sight of her as she came in and said to himself, *Hey, isn't this the girl in finance, the one who joined the same year as me? Shit, she looks so different.* He couldn't take her eyes off her as she walked in, looked around, and moved to the left of where he stood, her face wretched in a smile as she greeted somebody, and it wasn't very long before he sidled up to the threesome of guys she was with, trying hard to be conspicuously seen as contriving to join them. He picked up the threads of their conversation and soon mingled in quite smoothly.

It was about half hour later that he suddenly found himself alone with Rashmi. The other chaps had drifted away, two barwards. The one to speak with a colleague who had just come in. Ashok was normally an enthusiastic drinker, proud of his ability to hold the stuff. Today, with Rashmi next to him, he had slowed down. He had been on his second drink when she came in, and the glass was yet half full. Creating the right impression on her had suddenly become important.

'Would you like to sit down for a while?' he asked her.

'Yes,' she said. 'I am not used to these stand-up parties, and I must admit my legs are a bit tired.'

He led her to a quiet corner of the shamiana and sat her down and then strode up to the bar to get a refill for himself and a soft drink for her. For some time, after this day, they sat and talked about this and that that until, noticing that the music was on loud and that there were quite a few couples on the floor, he asked her if she would like to dance. 'Yes,' she said, and they were on the floor, facing each other, swaying gently to the rhythm of the music. *She moves so gracefully,* he thought to himself, *not like me, naturally clumsy me.* And then it was five minutes of twelve, and the music was changed to something soft and slow. Just about everyone was on the dance floor now, in readiness for the midnight ritual. Ashok looked at her tentatively, arms held ever so slightly apart, and she came to him without demur, and as he held her gently in his arms and tried to move as carefully as he could so as not to trample all over her poor little feet, he knew for sure, knew with certainly that this was *it*.

It was almost a year into time, the beginning to another Delhi winter. It had started to cool down, the air getting drier after the clammy months of July, August, and September. Most folks in the city, native Delhi dwellers included, seemed to live with the fantasy that it was just the months of May and June that were unbearable. That once the monsoon went in, the weather cooled off. Ashok had never agreed. 'A shame,' he had always said, too unlike his native Bombay where a good season of rain meant not seeing the sun for days. With the temperature in Delhi still in the high thirties, the combination of the heat and the humidity generated by the showers simulated a cauldron on a slow boil. Much worse than Bombay and with no sea breeze to provide some respite, at least in the evenings. The power cuts too seemed to peak out in this season. Spending half the night on the balcony outside his bedroom, clad in a pair of running shorts, fanning himself vigorously with the day's newspaper wasn't the most edifying of experiences, thank God, thought Ashok, for October.

Ashok and Rashmi had been seeing each other for almost ten months now. It was only last week that Ashok had popped the question and Rashmi had said yes, and he was yet a little disbelieving of the fact that she had consented. Disbelieving but joyous; they hadn't formally announced anything as yet because they were a little unsure of parental reactions. Ashok was Maharastrian, Rashmi of good Punjabi stock. All in good time. Not that either expected much opposition. And even if they did, they were consenting adults, after all. And in spite of the ethnic differentiation, their backgrounds seemed to each other to be extraordinarily similar middle class, unexciting but solid. Yet when he thought to himself, the one thing he still hadn't been able to figure out was why she worked in finance of all things, why she continued to work there. How could anyone possibly find any joy in crunching numbers and in balancing books? Their primary task seemed to be to criticize everyone else. Look at the fuss they had made last week about the trade discount that he had recommended as a part of the launch strategy for one or their new products. A lot of convoluted, meaningless calculations and they drew the conclusion that the erosion in margins wasn't affordable. What did these characters know about the realities of the marketplace, sitting in their cosy air-conditioned offices, hunched over their PCs and spreadsheets like so many gnomes, juggling their D-base programmes to get yet another sensitivity that would make sense only to them? The problem with these blokes in finance was that obscurity. Marketing was, after all, the cutting edge of the business, the people who slugged it out with the competition, the ones who brought in the money. Marketing was where the excitement was, where the results came from, not from that bunch of crummy bean counters. Rashmi was different, of course; she was a practical positive person unlike all those Cassandras. More importantly, she was an amiable disposition. *No wonder*, thought Ashok to himself. He just couldn't adjust to her being in finance where one of the prerequisites for membership seemed to be a surly temperament.

Ashok was on his way down the stairs in his apartment block, walking towards his motorbike parked below. He hadn't yet bought a car though he had been working for almost five years. He simply hadn't felt the need for it until now, and he wasn't a great one for keeping up with any Joneses. He was a quintessential Bombayite—thrifty, efficient, and businesslike. Ashok was still in the process of adjusting to Delhi, for it was so different from Bombay, so very different. The feeling of elbow room, for instance, still left him somewhat overwhelmed, used as he was to confined spaces, congested buses and trains, clogged traffic on the roads, and in general, a pace of life that would have left the average Delhiite thoroughly winded. He still recalled when he first moved to Delhi the unreal feeling of large vacant space that he experienced in what was a small *barsati* in Defence Colony. Now with a two-bedroom company lease in SDA, a sense of strangeness to him was the generally relaxed pace of life itself, where, for instance, he didn't have to rush from home to the railway station and catch a train that actually went two stops in the opposite direction and then returned the same way, else even standing space would have been impossible to come by. Many things were a pleasant change. Rashmi, especially. Yet sometimes he felt a twinge of longing for the bustle that was Bombay, for the evenings at Juhu eating bhelpuri and paav bhaji for the *bun maska*, dal fry, cold beer at the neighbourhood Irani, for the necklace of lights that was Marine Drive night, maybe more than anything else for the absolute, no-nonsense, businesslike culture that exemplified the city.

Delhi might be more laid-back, all right; living might be more comfortable in many ways. Yet in terms of efforts and reward, the one justifying the other, the other duly compensating the first, he wondered if it would come anywhere close to his hometown ever; no wonder the professors at his management institute often said that Bombay was the best breaking in ground for a marketing person. How true—what a difference there was between his first three years at the zonal sales office in Bombay and the last two years in Delhi; what really got him about Delhi was this boorish tendency to flaunt. As he often said to himself, earning a crore in Bombay was commonplace. No waves, just a quiet upping of lifestyle. The Delhiite, in similar circumstances, would probably tear down and rebuild the facade, mind you, the facade along his house, and invest in a couple of Toyotas. Mercs were out of fashion, he guessed, or more probably, out of reach.

It was while he was sipping a mid morning cup of tea that Vineet Sehgal told him that he had heard that the promotion lists would be cut that day. Vineet was barely two years into this his first job. He was carefree still and enjoying life, for the great rat race hadn't caught up with him yet. It would be another couple of years before the games of upward mobility along the organizational pyramid would start to affect him. For him, as for Ashok in his time, the first promotion would come fast and quick as long as performance was reasonable. It was then that the competition would start in earnest, and as one moved up the pyramid and the area around contracted in proportion to height achieved, the competing would give way to jockeying, the jockeying to a variety of political games, till at the very apex or near it, the knives often came out and petty skirmishes would often degenerate into prolonged wars. Ashok wasn't really due for a promotion this year. Maybe, looking at his performance, which he himself considered as extraordinary or close to it, he might find his name there. *But never mind*, he said to himself, *if it comes, it comes*. These things didn't bother him all that much.

There was a meeting with their ad agency later in the morning, and Ashok had promised to go over to their offices instead of their coming over as was usual. They had wanted him to have a first look at a number of visual ideas they had gotten ready for a new product launch, of which there were too many for them to conveniently bring over. He had said yes to going over and to lunch too.

Only sandwiches, please. He had a busy afternoon ahead back at the office, and heavy lunches only contributed to lethargy.

It was almost half past two when he got back. He found the office abuzz with conversation. The lists had been out barely ten minutes ago. Ashok was nonchalant about the whole thing, and it was almost a half hour later that he found the time to glance through the circular. No, his name was not there, and he hadn't expected to be. But what was this? Rashmi Tandon. He peered at the paper once again, just to make sure his eyes hadn't deceived him. No, they hadn't. The name started in the face from the bottom of the page. Well, he wasn't quite sure of how to react. Rashmi had been promoted. So what? She had probably done an excellent job of what she was supposed to, and that's why she had been. Not that he himself was doing too badly, yet she had been promoted and he hadn't been. Was she doing better than he was? Maybe. But finance! How could anyone there be better than a performer in marketing like him? Ineffectual people, to say the least, these folks in finance. No real contribution. But there it was, he said to himself, and he better accept it.

But he couldn't try as he did, he couldn't if he hadn't been promoted, and no one else from the batch that had joined the same year as he had been moved up; there wouldn't have been any cause for grouching. But was this fair? What had he not done over the past five years to be so unfairly overlooked? There had never been anything wrong ever at appraisal feedback time. Only unstinting praise. And look at the last major product launch six months back, all his brainwork. When to plan, almost with precision. What hadn't he done? This was the problem, he said to himself, with these Delhi companies. Didn't know how to appreciate talent, to reward performance. This wouldn't ever happen in Bombay. Guys there knew a person's worth. Really knew he had always felt unsure joining a company based in Delhi. Perhaps he should have listened a little better to his instincts and joined a Bombay outfit. This wouldn't have happened then. Five years, five full precious years of his working life. And what had come out of it? Nothing. Ashok felt cheated.

He didn't think his feelings for Rashmi had changed in any way. That was a different thing altogether. Why blame her? Poor thing, how was she responsible for the management's lopsided thinking? Of course, he congratulated her. And with genuine warmth. She accepted gracefully, except that he could sense that she was somewhat nonplussed at handling the situations. Almost apologetic about what had happened to her. After the bit of congratulating, she skilfully skirted the issue every time. But Ashok couldn't forget, couldn't get over the injustice of it that easily. He couldn't begin himself to be even remotely chagrined with Rashmi, and so his ire centred around two things that he had disliked mildly from the very beginning, this outfit where he worked and, even more, this alien city. He brooded a little. He moped some. Self-pity can, at its best, be a shade overwhelming. The more he brooded, the more his loathing increased. For the company, for Delhi. This pampered pseudo glamorous, unbusinesslike metropolis where the veneer of culture was so thin that the slightest scratch revealed the truth beneath. Of ostentatiousness, of mindless aggressiveness, very often of unscrupulousness. His discomfort grew and, with it, his dislike, and over the weeks, it bordered on something akin to an uncomprehending anathema. For both the company and for Delhi. It was difficult for him to decide which he disliked more.

And so he arrived at his decision, announced to Rashmi at lunch that Saturday afternoon. No talk on the promotion that hadn't come his way. Just that he had realized he didn't care very much for either the company or for Delhi. That five years in one and over two in the other were enough. That Bombay was a much better place for a career. More opportunities, a better working environment. That he loved Rashmi no less, that he couldn't possibly live without her. That he was sure that she would be willing to move. That they better announce their intentions to their respective parents soon. That his decision was, in a sense, final. Irrevocable.

Yes, Ashok had worried about how Rashmi would react. He loved her far, far too much to hurt her. Yet he knew that he had to go. Rashmi's response was cool, measured, almost noncommittal in a way that seemed to show to Ashok that she reacted to his decision, that she would probably stand by him. Yet it also seemed to indicate that she needed time to think. Never a reference to the promotion imbroglio, yet the underlay of what had transpired was definitely there. Unsaid, but definitely there. At one level he was somehow sure, convinced in his mind that she loved him, that she would follow, but at another, he was worried.

It was time for him to go about the serious business of finding himself a placement in Bombay. He would make a careful search, find something really suitable. He wasn't a flitty job hopper the way some of his friends were. Now that he had made the decision, he wasn't in a tearing, unthinking hurry. No way. He would take his own time about it, make a well-considered choice.

That evening, Ashok was off to the news vendor at the market near his house. He needed one more newspaper from the next day on, even though it arrived only in the evenings. Then he was off to the type shop two doors away for his biodata. It had an electronic typewriter, for which he was glad. Sunday morning, the clouds from his mind having slowly lifted, Ashok sat in his bedroom clad in a kurta and a pyjama, cross-legged on his bed, a half-forgotten cup of tea by his side, a small pair of scissors in his hand, assiduously snipping away at the employment ad page of the *Times of India,* Bombay edition.

* * *

A B-CLASS ABODE

The apartment that my employers, the bank, has provided me is comfortable, small, but Meera and I have been married only three months, and it is spacious enough for the two of us. The house faces a thickly wooded park, and I do enjoy my early morning cuppa and the *Times* sitting with Meera in companionable silence on the balcony that abuts our bedroom, the sports page and headlines in that order—important matters always take precedence. The city page is last priority, just a glance. I don't relate too well to rapes and murders and unidentified bodies, stabbings and shootings, kidnappings and bride burnings, which is what some of those who live in this large, sprawling metropolis seem to be doing to other residents on most days.

The two bodies that lay on the ground had been photographed from up close, which is why the faces caught my eye, surrounded by the trousered legs of policemen, thin, heavy-booted as they stood around the corpses. And one of the faces looked vaguely familiar. I knew him from someplace, I was sure of it. I was incredulous as my eyes shifted to the copy beneath. How, I asked myself, could I ever know one such as him, sprawled there in ungainly death? 'Unemployed graduate killed in shoot-out,' the headline read. And underneath, 'Surinder Singh, a university graduate who had turned to crime and was allegedly involved in over a dozen cases of kidnapping, was shot dead yesterday, in an encounter at village Ghazipur.'

* * *

I didn't have to attend class if I didn't want to. Actually go, you know, to an afternoon movie, just make sure that the wrong person didn't spot me, that the folks at home didn't get to know. And just imagine, three hours in the canteen if I so desired, idle my time away, converse, argue, tuck away a few samosas and cups of tea, smoke a surreptitious cigarette or two, ogle at the pretty young things who sometimes floated in and out. And what relief, I must admit, to be able to wear what I wanted to. Not that Papa and Mummy would permit anything outlandish, but reasonable freedom of choice all the same, which is better than khaki and white and nothing else for all those years at school. Knowing what it felt like to be suddenly unshackled, knowing because he'd probably have indulged in some or most of the same in his days, Papa is lenient. Up to a point. 'The best years of your life,' he'd said to me, 'enjoy them.' I am not saying you shouldn't. But be diligent too, learn where to draw the line for yourself, because in the end, if your scores aren't satisfactory, you know what's in store. A quiet chap, even-tempered, caring, but his eruptions can be likened to Krakatoa when they do occur once in a long while. Prudence in the circumstances is the name of the game, as it has been for the last few days. I study for up to sixteen hours a day, locked into my room, emerging briefly only at mealtimes for the final exams are just around the corner. And it has been reasonably smooth going all this while, everything in the right doses, everything to mutual satisfaction, Papa's and mine.

This sudden transition, boarding school to a local government-run college has its other sides too. For one, the unlikely, almost anthropological bemusement that emanates from encounters with people from sections of the social milieu with whom I have never had any contact, the confusion heightened from having been incarcerated for many years with peers of my own ilk, like-minded souls from fairly similar backgrounds. Disconcerting in some ways. As on my first day in class, I asked the person sitting next to me who he was and what his father did for a living, and he told me his name and said that his old man drove a truck for the Tatas, and I said to him, 'Now don't go around pulling my leg.' And he looked perplexed, couldn't comprehend my reaction, and fortunately I had enough of my wits about me to quickly carry the conversation on to something else, not let the bemusement turn into hurt. It took a while to adjust, but a year and a bit more into time and my assimilation was nearly complete.

Acquaintances, friends, relationships that varied from nod and hi to degrees of intimacy. I am not sure exactly where Surinder figured. Surinder Singh, to give you his full name. Somewhere in between, I guess, the enthusiasm a bit more from his side than mine. Let me explain why. Consider the fact that the only way he could complete his attendance quota was through a couple of hundred-rupee notes slipped quietly to the babu who was the archangel of the registers, else there was no earthly way that he would have been permitted to sit for any exam. And even when, in this fashion, he did manage to secure a hall ticket for himself, there wasn't a hope, he knew well enough, of his getting through. Unless someone helped. Which is where I came in, where a degree of befriending became for him almost an imperative. Not that I minded. A very useful person to know, especially in an ambience that was getting increasingly physical, often unruly. What, decades back, would have been rolled-up sleeves and fisticuffs over a girl's affections had now undergone an unhealthy metamorphosis into small-scale gang wars that had politics in the backdrop, a jostling for space and influence that often got out of hand. I kept meticulous miles away from anything that even vaguely resembled a fracas, but the possibility of being drawn into something unexpectedly, unwittingly, was always there, remotely at least. Which is why Surinder was always useful, as a prop in the background.

Surinder's personality was moulded significantly around a singular factor—the background which he had emerged from. The outskirts of the metropolis, where sizable tracts of land had, over the past couple of decades, been acquired and transformed into so-called farm dwellings—fairy tale structures set in the middle of landscaped gardens, heart-shaped swimming pools paved with pristine white Italian tiles, fountains and marble cherubs, lotus ponds and trimmed hedges, designer dwellings where the floor you walked on was quarried off the low hills that skirted Florence and Milan, no expense spared, the money spent on any such residence enough to support a normal middle-class existence for a generation or two in reasonable comfort. And to those families like Surinder's who had owned these hitherto sparsely cultivated, arid, dusty, acacia-throned, elephant-grassed, weaver bird-nested tracts for generations, the sudden, spurting demand for their joyless land was, any which way, an unlikely dream come true, providing jolting discontinuity to habits and lifestyles. And to those who had held on with sagacity, not tempted by the initial surge, what they now sat on was a gold mine. Literally.

Not much dearth of anything now in these once bleak suburbs, Maruti cars and vans, Tata Sumos, and the odd Cielo of late. Modest two- and three-room dwellings where once upon a time morning chores were performed on the dry fields outside, lota in hand, have now turned into residences considerably grander, with overstuffed laminate furniture, giant air coolers, and proper bathrooms. The only remnants that connect with the past are the stringed charpoys and ornate hookahs placed within courtyards where dried cow dung flooring has given way to pale-pink sandstone. This newfound affluence was reflected directly in Surinder's designer jeans, his neatly trimmed, longish hair, his aviator sunglasses with their pale-brown leather case threaded into his belt, and he drove into college on the odd day he deigned to put in an appearance in a newly acquired Zen, music at full blast, windows shaded in dark film turned up and the air conditioning on. Surinder's reputation preceded him, for he was ever willing for a rumbustious fight, in fact, seemed to revel in them, look forward to them, and though lean of build and seemingly scrawny of frame, he packed a mean punch. And he had built for himself a dubious reputation for audacity, for unbridled kick-in-the-privates aggressiveness easily provoked and, as a consequence, was treated with caution by most. He had built around him a small select group of committed, adoring acolytes—like-minded souls who swaggered similarly, his henchmen after a fashion. It was rarely, if at all, that he either created, or was dragged into, any serious trouble at the college itself, yet the stories of his exploits elsewhere abounded—inside restaurants, outside cinema halls, within newfound discotheques—ever confident that his clout, both economic and social, would be sufficient to bail him out of misdemeanours of reasonable magnitude.

As we approached our third year and the final finals, Surinder had accumulated a rather daunting backlog of papers, either not attempted or failed in. His exploits too had turned a shade nastier, and it seemed likely to me that the life ahead of him would, in all probability, be one that would verge itself on the fringes of the thin line of the law. And it seemed fairly certain that he would cross the line once in a while and end up on the wrong side of it. All this was, of course, the right training and qualifications for a natural entry into the great grey, murky terrain of electoral politics, a field that to me seemed the natural habitat for one of his disposition and temperament.

Which is why I was surprised one January morning when Surinder approached me at what was for him the unearthly hour of half past ten, for normally when he did come to college, it was only in the early afternoon.

'Will you have lunch with me?'

'Where?'

'I have an apartment now. Close by. I have hired it out for three months, till the exams are over.'

It was a furnished *barsati*, spartan, yet with all the very basic comforts attended to—also a kitchen and a cook to go with it. And the large table in the room that served as his living quarters was covered with stacks of books, economics, history, commerce, all the papers he had yet to finish with. I stared at the setting a little unbelievingly, and looked him in the eye, my expression begging an answer.

'I have got to get through,' he said. 'I simply have to.' There was a sense of urgency in his voice, a tone of purpose. 'Will you help me a little, please, when you can? Especially your notes. And if you can tell me what guide books to get. A few hours every week. Please.'

I consented, taken in by his earnestness.

And work he did, with a single-mindedness and assiduousness that amazed me. Arduous, the task in front of him, a near impossible one, for the portions to be covered were gargantuan. But pass he must, he impressed upon me repeatedly, get through somehow. Which I felt was the most optimistic that he could hope for, in any case. The sheer volume of work hitherto unattended was simply too large to run through in the time available for him to hope for anything but a scrape through.

And as the days went by, he displayed, to my astonishment, intelligence and an ability to comprehend that was far beyond what I had reckoned he would possess. I chipped in whenever I could, guided him through portions that were extra difficult to comprehend, advised him about what to focus on and what not to, where to take a chance and skip what I guessed was unlikely to figure in the exam papers. It was as if Surinder had imprisoned himself for the duration, for I don't think he ventured outside at all, nor was his band of ardent, fawning hangers-on permitted entry. And as D-day approached, he was palpably nervous, and sometimes when I visited him, he would be pacing furiously up and down the room, head bent towards open book in hand, muttering to himself.

It was fortunate for him that the very first paper he wrote was configured, as if by magic, to what he had focused on and learnt best. The resultant confidence helped him relax, which was important. Yes, on the odd day, he would seek me out, looking visibly disturbed, and he would tell me emphatically, a strong note of hopelessness in his voice, that there was no earthly chance of his getting through that particular paper.

On the day the last paper was written, he sought me out, hugged me warmly—half a dozen guys staring incredulously at the sight—and thanked me with sincerity for the assistance that I had been able to provide.

During the two-month interregnum of waiting for the results I didn't run into him at all. I was busy with the process of further admissions. I presumed that he had returned to his regular lifestyle, possibly living things up even more than usual, reacting with relief to the ending of his lengthy self-imposed hibernation.

On the day the results were to be published, I was there early enough, palpitating, preparing myself mentally for all possible downsides, hoping for the best all the same, confident one moment, sinking into an abyss of fear and desperation the next. When my scoresheets were handed over, I was pleased nevertheless, no nasty surprises. And as I walked out on to the corridor, grinning to myself, I had gone but a few yards forward when I heard a loud noise behind me and turned to see a person do a near bhangra as he came out the door, a beaming smile on his face, an admiring crowd watching him. Surinder, spotting me, ran to me, yelling, and clutching me by the waist, he lifted me to some height above the floor, amazingly wiry strength for someone so slim. Once his exuberance had subsided, he insisted that I spend one evening with him, dinner, and despite my attempts to wriggle out, he refused to take no for an answer. I was eventually persuaded, his sense of joy and relief drowning out whatever trepidation I might have experienced, trepidation arising out of the uncertainty of how an evening out on the town with him might end up.

* * *

It was an overly dimly lit place, laminated tables, chairs upholstered in synthetic leather, the decor startling shades of purple and green. There were imitation chandeliers hanging from an ornate plaster of Paris ceiling. There was a raised platform in the shape of a semicircle at one end of the hall by the far side of which a straggly-suited band of four was situated, two guitarists and a drummer and an individual with an oversized Casio. Their music was as ragged as they themselves physically looked to be, but their existence was secondary, almost of no consequence, I realized, as the first of the girls, overweight, puffy of face, caked make-up and an overdose of eyeshadow, a pasted grin on her face and a bored expression in her eyes, walked in through the curtains below and by the side of the stage. She climbed on to it and began to sway and jiggle. Rather gracelessly. This routine went on for fifteen minutes. Three more similarly built ladies had joined her on stage. All were all dressed in bikinis.

Surinder asked for a second Patiala. He insisted that my glass be refilled. He had a proprietorial air that said, 'Look at what a good time I am giving you!'

Surinder was into his second double double of RC whisky, topped with a bare minimum of ice and water; I was sipping a cold beer. He nudged me and winked, proprietary pride writ on his face as if he owned the place and the performers. 'Look what a good time I am giving you,' he seemed to be saying to me. When the band went offstage for a break and was replaced by piped music, the latest of local pop, Surinder thanked me once again. Graciously.

'But for you,' he said, 'there was no way I could have ever got through. I am grateful to you forever. If at any time there is anything you feel I can do for you, you only have to ask. I am always at your service.'

I was at a loss how to respond, for truthfully, I hadn't done much. It was the diligence that he had displayed, the single-minded purposiveness with which he had applied himself for those three months that had pulled him through. Which is what puzzled me. It was quite obvious that a career that would afford him a modest, decent living was not what he was looking for. Why then was this successful passage through graduation so important— almost a matter of life and death? An unlikely watershed for an individual such as him. I asked him. He fidgeted around for a few seconds and then replied in an undertone.

'It is a matter of looking out for myself. My future. Now that I am a graduate, you know the rules. I get B-class facilities in case I ever go into the lock-up. Imagine having to share a room with a dozen pimps and pickpockets and similar repugnant varieties. I wouldn't be able to do that. Never.'

* * *

PRINCIPLES AND THE PRICE LINE

*I*f you have travelled by train around the country, you would, I am sure, have encountered someone like Krishnaswamy. There are an even dozen of them on any of the mail trains that ply on the trunk routes. You can see them outside on the platform as the train boards, and you see the same faces inside as the train picks up speed, checking tickets and matching persons with berths and seats. They are attired, as always, in their black jackets—or at least what was black quite a while ago— now they are a patchy grey and stained with sweat and grime, the cuffs frayed, the buttons hanging loose, the edges wrinkled around the stitching. They mostly wear pale trousers and not-very-clean shirts and stringy ties of a nondescript black colour, their width never changing with changing fashions, instead exhibiting a resilient constancy. The final relics of the Raj when sweltering, heat notwithstanding, the sahibs still wore their linen jackets, starched collars, silk ties, and sola topis as they boarded their first-class coaches, away from the noise and the squalor of the natives.

Today the sahibs aren't there anymore. The more affluent of their ilk prefer to fly around. The ones you do encounter on the trains are of the unwashed variety, both themselves and their clothes. And they stink. Naturally. The pleasure is gone from rail travel nowadays, the exercise of securing tickets for any journey in itself an all-consuming nightmare. Add to that the beggars, the ticketless travellers, the food that is tasteless and of suspect hygiene, the chain pulling that gives you at least a dozen unscheduled stops per journey, the unclean WCs, and above all, the all-pervading stink that seems to pervade the entire railway system—a mixture of unwashed clothes, sweaty bodies, stale food, and even worse, the human refuse that lines the tracks. The AC bogies are a shade better, but not by much. The indolence, the relaxation, the enjoyment seems to have departed from the rail journey. Yet the Krishnaswamys remain constant, unchanging, clothed still in their incongruous jackets, these, the guardians of the reservation charts.

Their clout has increased exponentially over the years. The seats and berths are few, and the travellers are many. And increasing in numbers every day. A mere question of supply and demand. For Krishnaswamy, the temptations have been legion and hard to resist, especially if you consider what the Railways pays him. But he is not like the rest of them. He has his pride. He has his principles. He has a conscience. He also has a wife and three teenage children. A wife who demands, a wife who compares. The battle with himself to keep his honesty intact hasn't been easy. But Krishnaswamy has managed to—at least until now.

You must have seen many of those others standing outside their allotted coaches a full half hour before the train

leaves, a touch of the imperious to their postures, with
their clipboards and charts upon which they squiggle
mysteriously with pencil stubs tied to one corner of the
clip with a length of dirty brown string. You would have
seen them surrounded, often engulfed by supplicants,
those unfortunates on the waiting list. They seem so self-
important and always more than slightly irritated as the
cacophony of requests pours in all at the same time from
the semicircle in front of them. Yes, they have every right
to be irritated if this is what they have to go through every
day, considering the pittance they earn. But why is it then
that more than half a dozen wait-listers board the train
uninvited, especially when our man has been emphatically
telling them that there isn't an earthly chance of a berth
or a seat? The transactions occur almost an hour after
the train moves out of the station, after all the legitimate
passengers occupy their seats; they occur in and around
the small space that exists between the last row of seats
and the lav, most often near the now locked and bolted
door. Krishnaswamy has seen enough of it, knows the
kind of sums that change hands. Could range from ten
rupees in the slack season to as high as a hundred during
the summer vacations. No wonder that he is tempted. A
man can make an easy five hundred a month at the very
least off the top, and that is a lot of money. What couldn't
he do with that much extra? he has often thought. At least
it would shut his wife up.

*Maybe it is worth it, maybe my sense of values is out of tune
with the times*, says Krishnaswamy to his conscience as
he wheels his bicycle out of the staff cycle stand at the
far end of the station. *But I wouldn't know how to go
about it*, he admits to himself. He has no knowledge of
the nuances. Maybe he could ask one of his colleagues

to help. They'd fall off their seats from shock, he is sure. Not Krishnaswamy, they'd say to each other, not our own Gandhi. That is what they refer to him as behind his back. As if he doesn't know. Krishnaswamy is still engrossed in his thoughts as swinging on to his bicycle, clumsily steadying himself as he regains balance, he trundles his way along the road home.

Home to Krishnaswamy is a three-room semi-detached dwelling located in the second lane of the railway quarters, half a kilometre down the far side of the tracks. These small houses don't look too well maintained. They are a good half a century old in many cases and not very conveniently designed. Many of his colleagues have the money to do minor beautification on their own, but not Krishnaswamy. The broad green frontal wooden lattice that is a Railways signature has faded in the hot sun. The pale blue-tinged whitewash on the walls has been peeling off in long, thin flakes, aided no doubt by his children's ministrations. It has been four years since the house has had a coat of paint. The cement in the courtyard has chipped and cracked at various spots. Long, thin blades of grass thrust up through these crevices.

The courtyard has a small cement structure from the centre of which sprouts a rather straggly tulsi bush. The sitting room, which doubles up as a bedroom for the children at night, is furnished with hand-me-downs from his father's time. There is a plain wood-framed settee with cane back and seat, the wood lined with broad streaks of white and grey from not having seen polish ever since it was bought. There are two cane chairs, again last painted probably at the shop that made them, a fading pattern of red squares barely discernible on the inside of the back, the cane coming off in circular strands on the arms and legs, the legs so frail and bowed with age that they can hardly bear any weight. A bench, made long ago of good, seasoned wood and surprisingly heavy to carry, is placed against one wall. In the centre is their singular recent acquisition, a low table made of aluminium piping with a Formica-covered top, the colour a bright yellow and black. Two calendars hang on the wall, one belonging to the previous year. His wife had liked its picture-book portrait of the upper reaches of the Kashmir Valley in summer, of green meadows, snow-capped peaks and a clear blue lake in the distance, and had decided to let it stay. The other had Lakshmi on it, serene and four-armed, rising from a lotus in the middle of a lake. Ironical, because there wasn't a year when a calendar with her portrait wasn't there, yet its impact on their fortunes seemed minimal. As hand to mouth as ever. On the wall opposite the one bearing the calendars is a string of black-and-white photographs yellowed with age, of his parents in their youth, of his father in a turban, the ashes and sindoor on his forehead contrasted by a borrowed jacket and a thin silk tie knotted slightly off centre so that it hangs a shade askew. Of Krishnaswamy and his wife just after marriage, posing self-consciously at the local studio in their native town, elbows resting on a cylindrical wooden prop placed between them. One each of each of his children. And one of his father-in-law that his wife had put up, though his mother hadn't like the idea and had voiced as much.

As he comes in, he keeps a sharp lookout for his wife, twice his girth, twice his weight, and a voice many times his in decibel level. She is in the kitchen as he enters. He scrupulously avoids that area for he is looking for some respite, at least for some time. It is late afternoon. He picks up the *Hindu*—his one luxury—opened at the sports page by his cricket buff son and left that way, and begins reading. Srinath is almost seventeen but hasn't been up to very much of good through the years of early adulthood. Hair that to Krishnaswamy looks slightly weird in what his son terms as a step cut—the very latest, apparently, in follicular fashion. Krishnaswamy only knows that it costs him all of ten rupees each time, which is invariably once a month. That hurts, the ten rupees. At that age, the local barber used to cut his for four annas and so short that a further visit wasn't necessitated for at least two months. The no-good, spoilt wastrel. The singular subject both his wife and his mother agree upon. And mercilessly dote upon his every whim and fancy, straining Krishnaswamy's already stretched budget to near breaking point. If only he knew his maths as well as he did his cricket statistics! He's already dropped one class but it doesn't seem to bother him overly. How long can this go on? *I will have to put my foot down.* But Krishnaswamy knows he can't. The combination pitted against him is a shade too formidable. His wife and his mother. Together. God forbid! His two daughters, twelve and fourteen, aren't much trouble. They seem to be the only ones who care for him, who treat him with the affection, the respect, the dignity that he as the head of the household deserves. But what little they give is more than submerged in the ongoing tensions that rule the house, that seem to him so omnipresent and debilitating that he often fantasizes running away from it all. But where to? His wife, he is sure, will follow him to the ends of the earth and back. He is more than a little afraid of her, of her acerbic tongue, her seething sarcasms. More than anything else, he is afraid of her instinctive ability, when offended, of making life a slow, prolonged hell for him, knowing full well what irritated and provoked him the most. He was a nonentity in his own house, or near one, it seemed. He provided the money, of course. But considering what the others brought in that he didn't, it gave him little mileage. His only doubtful utility seemed to lie in his largely futile attempts at making peace between his wife and his mother. His mother, widowed, withered, and stooped with age, who, twenty years into time, still disapproves of the match that her husband had arranged for their eldest son. She had never approved of either her or her background. The resentment is still carried overtly, making the house a constant battleground, an ongoing, incessant volley of verbal snipers' shots whistling past Krishnaswamy's ears, causing him to duck mentally ever so often. His motto of peace with his wife, at any cost, is regretfully necessary for him to exist, yet it means having to put up with his mother's constant whining and with the enduring emotional blackmail when she refers to him variously as spineless, no man at all, his wife's obedient slave, and sometimes much worse when matters get really hot.

His brief, peaceful interlude with the *Hindu* for company doesn't last even all of five minutes, for his wife discovers that he is back. It is nearing the end of the month, and payday is still a week away. This is the time when the household budget is stretched so thin that the slightest jolt—even ten rupees of unplanned expenditure—would rend it asunder, leaving a gaping hole impossible to paper up. This is the time tensions run highest in the household, the time when his wife is at her virulent best. She starts off as soon as he sees him, as if some button has been pushed that activates her.

'How are we going to live this way?' she asks. 'And for how long? Yes, we have to scrimp and save and constantly tighten our belts. I can tolerate this if it is what fate has willed for me. I can, but how about the children? Do you imagine that they don't compare? Do you think that they don't realize what other fathers provide? Look at Balan. Do you know that Sumathi has got herself four new gold bangles? Do you know that Ramesh and Sangeeta have been bought brand-new clothes? What do you expect our children to feel? No, forget me. I can live with this. But look at your daughters—dressed as if they are from an orphanage or something. And Srinath, the rate at which he is growing, the way his trousers ride up above his ankles as if there are floods around . . .' and so on.

And on and on. The tirades seem never to end for Krishnaswamy. He removes himself as quickly as he possibly can from the house, going out just after tiffin on the excuse of meeting someone. He gets back only late in the evening, when he knows he can crawl into bed after a quick bite, feigning fatigue. He fidgets in bed, for his battle with his conscience continues unabated. Long years of constant fencing have left him inured somewhat. Looks like he is reaching the end of the battle. And his conscience is losing out. Surely he can't take much of this anymore, he tells himself. The reality of their existence, their heads barely above the subsistence line. The contrast that their neighbours so glaringly provide. He reluctantly admits to himself that there is some truth in what Alamelu spells out with such clarity during these tirades of hers.

The next morning, he escapes out of the house as early as he can after gulping down some idlis and watery sambar. He is coming to his decision and it troubles him no end. He goes to a movie theatre, the first time he has done so in months. His wife and his children are regular visitors, but he has normally refrained in the interest of whatever little money can be saved. It is a Sunday morning, the film a rerun of an old MGR blockbuster that in his youth would have had him on the edge of his seat as the hero missed death by a hair's breadth in varying situations. But today, tired, confused, and fretful, he merely closes his eyes and tries to shut out the noise as he fights the guilt that tears at him for what he is about to do that evening.

Yes, his father did retire an honest UDC in the revenue department with a reputation for integrity that sent him to his pyre in poverty, yet with his head held high. But what good had that done for the generation that succeeded him? Daughters married into indigence, sons in jobs such as Krishnaswamy's. At least in those days, a Brahmin could find a job on the basis of merit. Today even that was impossible, what with all the quotas and reservations. No, he wouldn't wish this job on his worst enemy. Maybe he was getting old, that is why the discomforts that had been for so long a part of his daily existence were getting to him. Sleeping three nights a week in a cramped half cubicle with the malodorous WCs opposite. Enduring the early-morning throat clearing by a procession of passengers into the small aluminium washbasin in the corner. All this for what?

He returns home around noon to find the house empty, except for his mother enjoying a siesta. Krishnaswamy helps himself to some food from the kitchen and then lies down for a nap. He is thankful for the quiet, but sleep does not come easily. He tosses and turns, fretful and restless. His train is at seven, and he gets ready to leave around six. As he passes his father's photograph in the drawing room on the way out, he averts his eyes, as if he might discover him staring back in righteous anger.

Both nervousness and guilt are rising in him as he reaches the platform at half past six. The crowds are milling around already. The ones with confirmations look confident and at ease; the others bow and scrape, plead and beseech. He better get into action, Krishnaswamy tells himself. Which of the ones looks a possible target? The fat one in the silk kurta looks a likely prospect. So does the young, fashionably dressed chap in jeans and a T-shirt. A half hour later, with the formalities of the chart completed, it is time for him to get into action. He catches the fat one's eye. Alert to the signal, the man waddles over to Krishnaswamy. This is the time of reckoning, the moment when the Rubicon has to be crossed.

'I am sure you can find me at least a seat, sir,' says the obese gentleman. 'Please, I will be most grateful.' Gratitude is the code for all such transactions, gratitude expressed in the form of two ten-rupee notes.

'I doubt it very much,' Krishnaswamy is supposed to say, 'but let me see.'

But no, at that very last moment, his nerve fails him. 'No, no,' he says. 'I can't help you. There are only four berths left, and there are over six people on the waiting list here already. Sorry.'

No, he tells himself, *I just can't. Don't be an imbecile. Do you want to endure this endless raving and ranting for the rest of your life, or do you want some peace? What values are you talking about? What principles? Forget your colleagues, don't the higher-ups make money? But no, not after twenty-five years.*

He knows that he will regret this cowardice the moment he gets home and his wife starts off. But he is happy deep inside that he hasn't compromised. Maybe there is a God out there who will help, eventually. And he turns his back on the man and starts calling out the names on the wait list.

And so this frail, small-made man in his jacket and tie stands, clipboard in hand, outside the sleeper coach that is in his charge. As the supplicants envelop him, he draws himself up a little firmer and straighter. This is that transient half hour when he comes into his own, possessed as if of a strange hauteur, straight-backed and regal in his bearing, when in the manner of Canute's fantasy the waves of humanity that surround him move as if to his will and command. That ephemeral half hour compensates for a lot. *I can live with all that and more*, he tells himself. *And not feel guilty either.*

* * *

Sharing a Berth

The ride in the auto rickshaw is long, and it chills me to my bones, all of ten kilometres from Panchsheel to New Delhi railway station. It is late January, around nine at night. Delhi is silent. The empty streets are dark and smoky, low-lying smog replenished each day by traffic emission and by the hundreds of open fires that the destitute, the homeless, have to depend on for a modicum of warmth. I discern action in pockets as we ride along, near the dhabas and the paan shops. CP is a wee bit livelier. The restaurants are open, but all shopping has ended at seven. Rambles is still populated, and so are some of the spots in the inner circle. A few cars ply; others are parked near the eating places. In the odd spots where people are gathered, I can see a smattering of three-piece suits, jeans, and pullovers. Thankfully, I am not subjected to the normal antics of the Delhi TSR driver who, at peak traffic time, can give you a heart-stopping journey as he weaves his way with perverse skill in and out of traffic lanes, missing other vehicles by bare inches or so it seems. Cultural adjustment problems, I have always said to myself, the transition from plying bullock carts through wide open, empty spaces to driving in an almost permanent state of vehicular claustrophobia.

That's when instinctive aggressiveness takes over. The whole city suffers from it, injected to it in large doses by those displaced folk from West Punjab, people who have left prosperous businesses and rich tracts of fertile land in Lahore and in Sind to start afresh in the refugee colonies of Delhi, barely a roof over their heads, surviving the first many years of resettlement by their initiative and wits and little else. I've often wondered what it would be like to be told that I can never go home again, that the place I call home with its mountains of verdant green, its endless coconut groves, its quiet, beautiful network of backwaters, is now going to be someone else's. Little wonder that Delhi's psyche is shaped the way it is. The instinct for survival knows no bounds, and the TSR driver epitomizes this instinct in a way; in this case, you ending up sharing the survival stakes, of course.

But I can't complain. The ride that night is easy, smooth. Except the last half a kilometre or so along State Entry before you turn into the railway station, when the road suddenly blossoms out into a row of brightly lit paan shops and eating houses that half encroach upon it and is suddenly filled with people. And tongas. And phutphutties. And the skilful weaving takes over, one hand on the horn all the time to make sure people scurry out of the way.

The couple of tots of rum that I consumed at my friend's place before dinner and departure seem to have evaporated during the ride. The sedative effect that I hoped for isn't going to be there. I sleep badly on trains. At six feet two, I don't seem to fit comfortably into the berths that they provide. If I lie with my head towards the window, my legs stretch out into the aisle, and they get knocked around and tripped over. If I put them the other way, it means folding them up double, and that isn't the most comfortable way to spend the night. *Never mind*, I tell myself, *I can catch up on sleep later*. I am slightly tense as I alight at the station for I don't possess a confirmed reservation. And that's bad going on Indian Railways, where wait lists don't often progress in correct sequential order. Agility and quick-wittedness are essential for getting on to the train under such circumstances, and the final ten minutes before the train moves out can leave you a minor nervous wreck. My travel agent has told me that number 5 on the wait list stands a good chance, and I console myself with the thought as I lug my suitcase along and jostle my way through the crowds at the entrance.

A medley of smells hits my nostrils as I move along, some pleasant, others decidedly disagreeable. But the mixture is what Indian railway stations are all about. Of unwashed bodies, of soiled clothes and bedrolls, of eggs panned into flat oily omelette stuffed liberally with onions and green chilly bits, of spiced tea ever boiling within large aluminium vessels placed over kerosene stoves that when pumped up, spew hot, fast-moving flame. There are people everywhere, all shapes and sizes, all hues and shades. Farmers in dhotis, kurtas, and turbans squatting on their haunches, wrapped up in rough woollen blankets. Women in silk and pashmina. Army men on furlough in olive green and khaki. City menfolk in suits, loud jackets, wind cheaters, pullovers. All of them, it seems to me, are talking at the same time, for the decibel level is at a constant high in the background. Up the stairs, slightly winded from my twenty cigarettes a day and the suitcase that I am carrying, a long trudge along the raised walkway that spans the rails and down to the platform at the far end and the Dehra Dun Express.

The Delhi-Kota bogies are already on the platform, awaiting the incoming train from Dehra Dun to which they will be joined, to be detached once again at Kota as the train moves on westward to Bombay. I look for the railwayman with the reservation chart. There he is, small and pompous, black jacket and thin twisted tie knotted a couple of inches lower than the collar, the shirt covered with an incongruously colourful half sweater of blue and purple that his wife must have clicked away at for weeks. I mentally confer upon him an odd sense of dignity despite his unlikely sense of dress, for he has the power tonight to decide whether I board the train or no. He has already been mobbed by a dozen weightlifters like me and looks more than slightly irritated. It shows in his voice as I elbow my way through the semicircle in front of him, putting my height, weight, and reach to good use.

'Fifth on the list,' I tell him.

'Wait, wait. There is a full half hour left.'

'Am I still at number five?' I ask him. 'Rajgopal.'

'Yes. There haven't been any cancellations.'

'What are my chances?' I ask.

'I can't tell you now. I told you to wait, didn't I?'

No use standing here, I tell myself. *I can elbow my way back in later*. I stride up to the A. H. Wheeler nearby. Higginbotham and Wheeler. The Indian Railways bookstore staples. The first down south, the second up north. Good Anglo-Saxon names that resonate with the ring of the Raj. I am an Anglophile at heart. I pick up a couple of magazines as an insomnia antidote and walk aimlessly around for a while, smoking a cigarette. And then back to the little man and his anxious audience. It is another five minutes before he speaks, and then it is to say that there are only two berths vacant.

'Mr Kumar,' he calls out. A plump man dressed all in white—pullover, trousers, and shoes (golden buckles, I notice)—steps forward. A well-fed, well-powdered look about him, a thin line of a moustache on his upper lip looking as if it were painted on, hair very obviously dyed and unreal black, the roots showing grey white underneath. I dislike the look of him, detest him for being there. The little man squiggles mysteriously on the ticket proffered to him and again on his chart. Mr Kumar looks eminently pleased with himself, strangely like an overweight Pomeranian that severely lacks exercise. *A pom with its head dyed black, of course*, I say to myself a shade viciously.

'Mr Luthra.'

This one has a receding hairline that he is desperate to cover up, pulling long strands of hair from one side of his scalp and combing them over it to the other side. From my height, the view is faintly ridiculous, for he is a good six inches shorter than me. The only guys who he might fool with this self-designed natural wig are folks a good deal shorter than him, if at all. Mysterious squiggling once again, and the little man looks up with an air of finality.

'The wait list is closed,' he proclaims.

Officially, that is. No one seems to take him very seriously. Several side up and engage him in whispered conversation. I know I am no good at this sort of thing. Wouldn't know how to. I go up to him and peer down at him, look him straight in the eye, look as contrite as possible.

'Any chance at all?' The tone is full of clever implication of future reward, or so I like to think.

'I told you the wait list is closed, didn't I?' He dismisses me brusquely. Maybe he dislikes tall people. I suffer from the inverted snobbery all us tall guys have, especially in a country such as ours where average male height is under five feet five. I remember reading that somewhere. The statistics, I mean. *Short bastard*, I say to myself. *And sod my travel agent. Good chance, my foot. Hope Ashok hasn't gone to bed yet. Would be terrible having to wake him up.*

As I turn to go, I see a vaguely familiar figure alighting from the compartment that I was supposed to board and beckoning to me. It takes me a moment or two to place him. He is my neighbour from the *barsati* upstairs of my ground floor flat in Kota. He had moved in about a month back. I recall his name with some difficulty. Umesh. He is as reclusive as my flatmate and I are boisterous, a quiet chap who keeps to himself. He works in the factory next door to the one where I am employed. I know him very slightly, if one could even call it that. But he seems friendly enough as he walks up to me.

'Any problem?' he asks.

'Not really,' I tell him. 'No chance of a berth tonight. Maybe I'll try the Frontier tomorrow.' That is a day train that reaches Kota late evening. The Dehra Dun is more convenient—an overnight journey and you don't waste working time.

'Don't be silly,' he says. 'I have a confirmed reservation. Why don't you pile in with me?'

'No, yaar. I don't want to hassle you. I'll try tomorrow.'

'No problems, I assure you. Not from my side. It's only a ten-hour run after all. And I have a lower berth.'

Umesh is well below the national average, five feet two or thereabouts. I consider the possibility. The idea is physically feasible, but what of the pompous ass in the black jacket? I have that to consider.

'The TTR might hassle us,' I tell Umesh. 'He seemed a cussed kind of chap. I don't want to create unnecessary trouble for you.'

'You don't actually believe that, do you? That the guy can't be managed? Don't worry, I'll take care of it. Come along and stop worrying.'

A quiet chap with an utterly unassuming air about him, you couldn't have believed it. 'Full many a gem,' as the poet said. I am persuaded. I follow him into the compartment and sit down next to him on the seat that will be pulled out and made our bed later on. The guy bound for the upper berth who is already seated by the window looks at Umesh enquiringly.

'He'll be sharing my berth with me,' Umesh tells him.

Ten minutes later, as the train moves out, we are smoking and making desultory small talk, for we don't have much to say to each other. My tension is still there, for the ticket-checking hurdle is yet to be crossed. I'm depending on Umesh's panache. The pompous little man from the platform arrives on the scene around fifteen minutes later. He recognizes me from the platform and gives me a plainly aggressive glare.

'Do you have confirmed reservation?' he snaps at me.

I told you, the guy hates me because I'm so much taller. I'm unsure of how to reply. There are already three of us sitting on the berth when there ought to have been only two. If I say yes, he will ask me for my ticket; saying no is asking for trouble straight off. I look at Umesh out of the corner of my eye, a shade helplessly. He comes to the rescue, brave soul. A tenner, apparently secreted in advance in his pocket, appears as if by magic in the palm of his hand, visible to the little man.

'He isn't asking for a separate berth. He will share mine with me,' declares Umesh.

Umesh hands his ticket over for checking, and the tenner changes hands too. Some magician, this. It works. It does! The guy moves on. My tension evaporates. I stretch my legs and light up a cigarette. We continue with our aimless conversation. Umesh isn't a sullen sort, no. Pleasant enough. It's just that he doesn't say much. A little later, he opens his bag and pulls out a small cardboard box wrapped in a brown paper packet, the kind in which the Delhi shops pack mithai. Gaily printed top and white base. He opens it and offers it to me. Parathas with aloo sabzi inside, neatly rolled up for easy eating. There is a generous helping of pickle tucked away at one side of the box. I tell him that I've already had a bite before starting off for the station. He is quietly persuasive.

'My mother always insists on packing for more than I can eat. She feels it's her bounden duty to feed me up. I'm an only child, you see. Thinks I'm far too thin. *Half starved* is the way she puts it. I mean the way she thinks I look.'

He is thin, all right. I'm any only child too. Not that I have had problems of being underweight. Not in a long time at least. Quite the reverse. The food smells good, and I am not that full either.

'Just one,' I tell him. 'Thanks.' I help myself to a roll and a generous daubing of pickle. Delicious. I end up having one more, feeling slightly guilty. But Umesh doesn't look deprived. There's one still left over when he is through. He raises the window and chucks the packet out. We wash up at the small basin beyond the last berth, to the side and front of the WCs, and return to our seat. The occupant of the upper berth has climbed up quite some time back and is now sound asleep, snoring ever so softly, a slight purring sound. *Lucky chap*, I tell myself, *that he can sleep so well*. One more cigarette, smoked in silence.

'Shall we sleep?' Umesh asks me.

'Yes,' I reply. 'Sorry about this once again. I hope I won't keep you awake.'

'I sleep very soundly,' he tells me. 'An earthquake wouldn't wake me. You don't have to feel guilty.'

I hope that's the truth, for his sake, knowing what a restless sleeper I am. And so to bed fully clothed, his feet near my head, my legs doubled up against the window sill near his. His feet don't stink. I don't know if mine do. Even if they do, he suffers in silence, I suppose.

An unusually restful night for me. I wake up only minutes before the train reaches Kota, and that too after some energetic prodding from Umesh. We are out of the station and into a TSR, the Kota variety, slightly less audacious in driving style than his cousins in Delhi but not by much. We are home in fifteen minutes. I insist on paying the driver, won't let Umesh share. Quiet persuasion on his part doesn't work this time. I am adamant. Least I can do for him, I suppose. My house help is at the gate, awaiting my arrival. He takes my bag from me as Umesh turns to go up the stairs.

'Why don't you come down and have breakfast before you go to work?' I ask.

'No,' says Umesh. 'I'm in a bit of a hurry. Thanks anyway.'

I bathe and am finishing breakfast when out of the corner of my eye, I glimpse a figure on the narrow cemented drive by the side of our house. I turn around to see better. It is Umesh, pushing his scooter. I go out and ask him what the problem is.

'Something wrong. It isn't starting. I'll drop it at the mechanic's.'

'Why don't you leave it here?' I tell him. 'I'll give you a lift.'

'No thanks,' he says. 'There's lots wrong with it. I was planning to give it in to the garage anyway. And I have a few chores to complete after that. You go ahead. See you later sometime.' He pushes his scooter on to the road and walks along slowly to his mechanic's workshop, situated not very far away.

And that is the last time I saw him, for Umesh died. That very morning, riding to the factory in a TSR that took too sharp a turn to avoid a pothole, overturning and throwing Umesh out of the vehicle. And a truck speeding in the opposite direction couldn't stop in time and ran over him. Yes, he died barely an hour after I last saw him pushing his scooter. Disbelief. Shock. Guilt. All gnawed at me simultaneously. That I had deprived him of that last night's rest or at least disturbed it. That I should have insisted that he had breakfast. That I should have forced him to take a lift with me. The thought of his parents' grief. All that was there.

But there was something else too. Something I couldn't quite put my finger on. Something that I ought to be ashamed of; I knew that as if by some instinct. That night, as I lay down in bed, restless, I ran the previous evening through in my mind. Our meeting on the platform, our conversation as the train moved out. His sleight of hand with the little man. And then it came to me. Incongruous. Absurd. But a shame, all right. A shame I have always lived with. For I owed him that tenner.

* * *

DELHI DURBAR

'*Y*ou don't actually mean to say you take them seriously, do you?'

Vipin sounds slightly irritated. He realizes that he does, but he isn't apologetic. Not in the least. Irritation is what a question as inane as the one Rajinder has just put to him deserves. Imagine taking these pronouncements seriously! What is wrong with him?

Rajinder had asked him a little while ago, 'Do you think they are serious this time? All this talk of major policy changes and less control?'

The two of them are in the canteen on the ground floor of the office block of this building that must have been roomy and majestic in its time, now more than a shade seedy, the result of a combination of apathy and studied neglect. The place is crowded at that hour, and they are sharing their table with four others, two known to them slightly, two strangers, probably visitors. The table has thin steel legs, painted black many seasons ago, and a white Formica top, now greyed and yellowed and stained in many colours. It wobbles slightly as Vipin presses the top with his palm in emphasis of his pronouncements.

The place is crowded at that hour, the dozen or so tables all occupied, cups of tea and coffee moving in from the kitchen on loaded trays.

'You know what governments are like,' he says. 'This is a part of political routine. They ride in on a wave of euphoria, and at that point in time, they feel very good about themselves, and it's almost compulsive. This saying the right things. I mean you can't have a new government coming in and making no pronouncements, can you? Tell me, can you? They ride in on a promise of change, so they have to. Utter these inanities, I mean. But take them seriously? You must be out of your mind.'

Vipin pauses for a second or two to sip his tea served in a coffee mug chipped along the mouth, the handle missing except for a remnant of curved stub that protrudes on the side, and he has to cup it delicately with his palms, delicately because the tea served is hot, near tasteless but piping hot. 'Remember Rajiv Gandhi?' he continues. '1985. Four-hundred-plus seats. "I'll clean up the Congress Party," he said. "I'll eliminate all the power brokers." Mr Clean. And what happened in the end? They cleaned him out, didn't they? Cleaned him out and converted him, and things were back to the good old days.'

'I agree,' says Rajinder, 'but this time it seems a little different. They are being much more specific, and they are indicating dates too. No general statements. That is why I get this feeling that perhaps they are a little more serious.'

'It will be like committing suicide, let me tell you. None of them is fool enough to do that. The whole thing is too intertwined, Rajinder. It is a full circle and hard to breach. The interests are dug in too deep for anything to really happen. I mean, people like us are small fry. Extremely small. Okay, some of us make small amounts of pocket money on the side. I am not pretending that doesn't happen. But what of the big fish up there? Three per cent into a Swiss bank, half for themselves, half for the party. And we are talking of thousands of crores. Three per cent of that is a lot of money.' Vipin pauses to sip his tea. 'Can they ever fight elections without that money? The whole system is too intricate for anyone to be able to unravel it now, my friend.'

Vipin glances at his watch. It is fifteen minutes to closing time. He swallows the last of his tea and pushes his chair back.

'Come, let us get back,' he tells Rajinder. That's normal routine, a half hour tête-à-tête in the canteen in the evening. Especially so in the winter, when the sun sets early and the cold seeps into their bones in the high-ceilinged room in which they sit and work and the rod heaters that are standard government issue seem to provide no respite. A cup of tea is welcome. As they climb the stairs, Vipin places his packet of cigarettes back into the inside pocket of his blazer, a blue-black Raymonds ready-made with shiny brass buttons and quality silk lining. Had cost him all of eighteen hundred but worth every rupee. Vipin believes in living well, and not just for himself but for his family too, unlike a lot of his colleagues who spend all the money on themselves, most of it on liquor and on stag dinners five days a week. Okay, so he likes dressing well and smokes only India Kings at twenty-five for a packet of twenties and used a posh black-and-gold lighter, but the last named was a gift from one of the droves of liaison types who floated in and out of his office, and yes, it looked really smart. And he enjoys his smokes, but that doesn't mean that he doesn't care for his family. He gives them a good life, yes he does. Today, for instance, is a Friday, and he has promised Sangeeta and Sandeep dinner at the Delhi Durbar in CP, no less, for Sandeep loves their butter chicken, and they serve beer, and that makes Vipin happy too.

The meal will probably set him back three or four hundred rupees, but so what? He is only forty-two. He has sixteen long years left, and the system is well-oiled, and he accepts that the income does fluctuate a bit seasonally, but on the whole, things are more than comfortable. And import licenses and duty drawback claims aren't going to go out of fashion, not that easily in any case. Too much is centred around their issuance and what goes almost naturally with it. And that's why he believes in living life well. A two-year-old Maruti and decent furniture and new curtains every three years or so and a Sony TV. Sangeeta can't complain. No flashiness of course. Subdued well-being. Conspicuousness attracts unnecessary envy, and that can lead up to all manner of unpleasant happenings, which is the last thing he wants. Hence a degree at least of austerity is essential.

Yet as he sits in the bus and watches the tree-lined avenues of South Delhi pass by, the air smoky with the smog that has settled in early in the evening, a degree of disquiet rests in him, deep within his mind, and try as he might to suppress it, little bits of it surface into his consciousness, and he can't shake those traces off. He attempts to laugh at himself for thinking such thoughts and says to himself, *It's all rhetoric, now don't you start taking them seriously.* People like Rajinder are bad enough.

Life is good, Vipin says to himself emphatically as the bus stops at the traffic light before it turns towards the road on which the block of apartments where he lives is situated, Jawahar Lai Nehru Stadium towering in the foreground on the left. If only he could get them an air conditioner, even summer would be perfect then, especially July and August, for a cooler was fine until then. But he daren't, for that is the easiest route to being noticed. Maybe they could move to the three-room set that they had acquired at Rohini, away from prying eyes. But that would mean that the rent would stop coming in, and besides, Lodhi is so convenient for all of them, and Sangeeta's school where she teaches is just a ten-minute bus ride away. And Sandeep's school is close by too. Costs him all of five hundred a month if he adds up all the little bits, but he believes in giving Sandeep the best, giving him a head start in life, not like himself a government school and Khalsa.

The buildings form a three-storied rectangle of windows and tiny balconies, a rectangle with gaps at the four corners for passage. A cricket game is going on in the dying light in the quadrangle in the middle, and he can see Sandeep in the distance. He waves to him as he enters the stairwell. Sangeeta has spotted his approach and opens the door even before he rings the call bell and, as he deposits his briefcase and a video cassette in the bedroom, busies herself in the kitchen, boiling water for tea.

'I've got *Tridev*,' he yells to her. 'We'll watch it after we get back.' She'd wanted to watch it at Odeon, but he'd put his foot down, what with terrorists and bomb scares and all the rest of it. He'd bought the *Midday* at one of the traffic lights where his bus had stopped, and it had been too dark to read on the bus. He settles down on the sofa, part of an upholstered set, a three-seater and two singles that they had picked up for a bargain at Panchkuia Road with carved legs and velvet fabric. He glances through the headlines as Sangeeta places his tea on the table in the centre, a new Hitkari set with deep purple flowers running around the cup, none of the chipped variety that he gets in the office. And she stands behind him and peers at the paper.

'Commerce Minister promises speedy liberalization. Will simplify import–export procedures. Partial convertibility.'

And Sangeeta is intelligent and aware, and more than that, there has been talk at school in the staff room, and she realizes what those headlines might imply, and it's been going on for so many days, and maybe this is the right time to ask him.

'What will happen,' she asks, 'if they implement all this that they have been promising?'

And Vipin has a strange look in his eyes as he turns to her and he says, 'Don't be silly, Sangeeta. They won't. This is what every new government does. You know that.'

And he tells her, 'Better call Sandeep in and ask him to bathe and change. It's six already. Remember, we are going out for dinner today.'

* * *

THE INHERITANCE

I am almost tempted to say 'Never again!' Let me qualify that. The winter might yet be tolerable. But not summer. I didn't know what I was letting myself into, surely not, else I might have chickened out. I mean, I always did have a choice. Which is why, when I look at it, my predicament seems to have more than a touch of the ludicrous. Even a year back, the probability didn't exist, or at least it hadn't occurred to me. But that is the way it is with us, I suppose. A legacy is a legacy and rightfully yours, so better lay claim to it, else it might just wither away or, worse still, pass into alien hands from which retrieval would be a near impossibility, which is why I had to. And my mother pushed me, of course. Mummy is earthy, shrewd, practical. I put up token resistance but yielded in the end, just as I probably knew I would when it began.

Maybe, come to think of it, I always knew that this was going to happen. Not that I consciously accepted the reality of it or ever savoured the thought with relish. Yet somewhere within the recesses of my mind, the possibility must always have been there, this underlay of foreordination, this being drawn into something that in one sense I was unprepared for, that went against my essential predisposition, my grain, my temperament. How incongruous, you might say, or, if you didn't pull your punches, how hypocritical. When you've lived with the reflection of the pomp and the glory, the power, enjoyed its trappings for so long, how can it be? That you too wouldn't aspire to all that and perhaps a little more? But honest to goodness, I didn't. That's the truth as I best experienced it.

Maybe it is because everything had been there since I care to remember; maybe I took things for granted, the golden-spoon principle, without meaning to sound uppity. And it's only a combination of events like this, unexpected, ill-timed, a chance in a million, so to say, by the normal laws of averages, that throws everything out of gear so comprehensively that the rest of the sequence acquires a shade of inexorability when choices evaporate, when you are sucked into the vortex, when your whole life changes. And mine changed in a period of time that by normal standards of measurement was long but which to me, as I lived through it, felt like a millisecond, a millisecond when I was fighting the swirling waters that were closing over me and I was thrashing about in a last act of desperation, saying to myself, *I can't, I can't, I won't*, and I found myself conscious in a coarse-spun khadi kurta pyjama, the string tied a shade too tight and cutting into the thin wedge of flab that I had accumulated around the gut.

I didn't know that khadi could be so prickly, especially when starched. But I know I have to wear it, for white khadi is a part of the uniform. Thank goodness you get them ready-made. Twenty pairs is what I've had to buy for a start. I said why twenty? Shades of Bertram Wooster.

'You'll live and learn, baba, you'll live and learn.' Mummy has a habit of repeating herself in speech, perhaps with an intention to emphasize.

And I have learnt a lot since I said yes. I mean, sadistic. The circumstances. And masochistic. The volunteering. The dyad is lethal, as you can imagine. Forty-four in the shade. Celsius, not Fahrenheit. Dry, my foot. Forty per cent humidity? Not when you have two-score human beings whirling around you constantly like so many dervishes. I alternately sweat and dry up until I feel as if I am being salted away.

It was in March that my father died. And he went so suddenly, it seemed, for he had looked so much younger than his three scores and ten. The late fifties is what you could have best labelled him at if you considered the externals. It's the adrenaline, I suppose, an almost continuous flow of it into the bloodstream. And the phenomenon has a certain universality about it—all the worlds, the first and the second and the third, the whites, the browns, the yellows, the blacks. It's the same everywhere. The fountain of eternal youth, or of middle age at least, which isn't bad going. But the body ages though the exterior doesn't. And that's what happened to him, I guess, amidst all the excitement of one government going, of another coming, of the continuous being on the edge, of the adroit acts of brinkmanship that followed, when the acrobatics were breathtaking for a lay spectator and to the deeply involved, even heart-stopping. And his did. The excitement, the audacity of the high-wire act, the tension, were a little too much for even someone who had been through this many times. And his heart stopped suddenly, no prior notice. Abrupt way to go. And almost at once, the pressure came on. At that point I still had time to think, or so I thought to myself in my naivety, for the Houdini act looked like it wouldn't end, at least not that easily. No one seemed to want it to. And so I breathed easy for a couple of weeks until the Haryana constable sequence, and that's when I hit quicksand, that is, when the horizon grew inevitably closer, nearer the tip of my nose, if you please. That's when it became a now-or-never thing and it had to be now or else, as Mummy put it, it could very well be never.

My Hindi was good, or so I had always thought. But speechifying in it is very different, as I discovered for myself. Painfully. I'd rather not remember the first time, after filing my nomination. Initialization day, so to speak, for I'd finally given in just a day before. Let me not get into that. My wife on the one side, my mother on the other. That says it all, doesn't it? But an inheritance is an inheritance. Not to be squandered away. That says it all too. And that's when Usha starts feeling she's the sacrificial goat at the altar of the bloodlines. Picturesque way of putting it, but she was always good with words, unlike my Hindustani, as I'm beginning to find out. Yet the crowds bear with me, for I am his son. He of the four terms, possibly a fifth, had he lived. They are patient, forgiving. And curious. And they listen to me. I am truly amazed. I sign the papers placed in front of me, sitting on a rickety wooden chair in front of the returning officer. I have this feeling of being smothered for there are as many people behind me as the room can hold—standing, jostling, talking, a continuous subdued hum, the decibel level low in deference to the solemnity of the occasion. A burfi is thrust into my mouth from a newly opened box. It is a pale green in colour. Heaven knows where it was made. Hope I don't land up with the trots, I tell myself. They could have given me some notice, some warning that I would have to speak. Maybe Chater Lal ji took it for granted that I would know the sequence. Anyway, I am ushered out of the room, manoeuvred towards the large courtyard outside of the building, and placed in front a pair of microphones through which Chatar Lal ji shouts, 'Chaudhary Rajiv Singh, zindabad! Chaudhary Raghbir Singh, amar rahe!' And the crowd responds in unison, with gusto. That's a new one. Rajiv, Raju, Mr Singh. Rags to my intimates in Boston. Chaudhary is a new one.

'And now our beloved candidate, Chaudhary Rajiv Singh, will say a few words of encouragement, of guidance. Chaudhary Rajiv Singh, zindabad!'

The crowd echoes the chant once again. I peer closely at them for the first time. They are my frontline of support, the spearhead of my campaign. How motley can you get? Some of the faces upfront are vaguely familiar—my father's last rites, I guess. Most of the rest present a disconcerting collection of the unshaven, the swarthy, the ill-dressed, types you would scrupulously avoid on a lonely night walking down an unlit street. All of them are craning their necks, standing on tiptoe, trying to get a good look at me. They are waiting for me to say something, but I am tongue-tied. I kick myself mentally. Think fast, for Chrissakes. The sweat is breaking out on my brow and on the nape of my neck just below the hairline, pouring down in streams. And I can feel the knot of pyjama string coming slightly undone, not enough for it to collapse around me, God forbid, but quite enough to distract. They are waiting still for me to begin. Patiently.

'My beloved friends,' I start off tentatively. 'Thank you for your encouragement and support.' The party. I better say something about the powers that be. Not that they had much of a choice either once I had decided to say yes. 'I thank the party central committee for giving me the honour of fighting on their ticket.' *Good line*, I tell myself. *Central committee* is in English. I haven't the faintest idea of what the Hindi equivalent is. But it seems to have gone down well enough. The old man has to figure now, I tell myself. 'I hope and pray that I will live up to your expectations, that I will be worthy of my father's name. Thank you. Jai Hind.'

Short and sweet. Very good, my dear boy, very good. Sherwood Hall should be proud of you. I was always a natural when it came to debating. But the tension has been overwhelming. I feel a little faint as I am escorted through the jostling crowd, people reaching out to touch me, tugging at my kurta. Not my pyjamas, please, they might slip off any moment. My white Ambassador—part of the uniform—is parked to the side near the gate. Ram Vilas has been sensible. The engine has been kept running; the inside is cool. Thank heavens for air conditioning. I am whisked away homeward.

That is just the beginning, a brief foretaste. Three weeks of it. Three godawful weeks. I am just not used to the heat anymore. The six years in New England have spoilt me, and the year back home in New Delhi hasn't been uncomfortable either. A cosy suite of adequately air-conditioned rooms in the ministerial residence, for they didn't force us to move during the fifteen-month hiatus of my old man being out of office. And my software outfit was just starting to take shape, the first large export order recently tied up, when all this had to happen, this maelstrom of events that sucked me into its epicentre. My karma. I am trying to take a philosophical view of things. I need to, else my equilibrium will go to pieces, for the pace is gruelling. Usha has refused to be a part of all this, is still in a fair sulk, ensconced in faraway Delhi. Someone has to run the agency, I suppose. What if I don't make it in the end?

The Shri Ram battalions are going to give me a fair run for my money, I am told. But they are slightly handicapped. It's rather like a boxing match with one hand tied behind the back, poor chaps. I use my old man's name freely; in fact, that's the main plank for me. But they can't speak ill of him, not so soon after. Not done in these parts, where only the bad is interred with the bones. The good lives on, for a while at least. There's not much to be said about me either way. And I am my father's son. That seems to be enough. For now. The next time around, I know it's going to be tougher. I'll be me then, shed of his halo. The two factors that favour me, sympathy and curiosity, would have evaporated. I am slowly beginning to comprehend Mummy's hurry, her motivations.

But it's no cakewalk, let me assure you. 'Jai Shriram. Jai Bajrang Bali.' And strident promises that the temple would be built. Whatever the cost.

The temple is the icon, the magnet that they hope will attract the votes. The frenzy is building up as D-day approaches. Scores of the saffron clad are fanning out into the villages, visible in increasing numbers as we drive along each day. There isn't much I can do. Wide coverage is the only possible answer. And 'Chaudhary Raghbir Singh amar rahe.' No, I am not being sardonic.

The pace is hectic. Up at six and an hour and a half to myself. Half past seven, it is breakfast and my strategic plan meeting if you may call it that. A closed inner circle. Chatar Lal ji is always there, and Mummy. And any special invitees they chose to so honour. It starts with the day's schedule. I am learning, absorbing fast. The friendly pockets, the unfriendly ones. What to say where, how to bring the old man in, emphasize what he's done, what he's accomplished. The budget is next. Posters, banners, petrol, food for my phalanx, dole for each of them for the day. I am shocked at first. If this is what we are spending—and from the looks of it, the Ram Sevaks are spending even more—what must it all be adding up to? I begin to appreciate the subterranean economy a little better, the need for it to be the way it is, the manner in which it supplies the very lifeblood to our political system.

'Khajaria has always been dicey,' intones Chatar Lal ji. 'They can swing either way. The ungrateful so-and-sos.' My mother nods her head in agreement. 'It is important, Chaudharyji, that we have at least one good meeting there. The evening is best, say around six thirty. That's when we can draw the largest crowds. I'm sending Sukhdev over in the morning itself to make sure that things are organized properly. And respected late Chaudharyji has done a lot for them. The community hall, the veterinary clinic. You must emphasize that. I'll remind you before the meeting.'

I nod my head gravely. Chatar Lal ji is my walking encyclopaedia as far as the constituency goes. I remember him ever since I can remember, to put it simply, a cousin twice removed of my father's but more than that, my father's major-domo, secretary, treasurer all rolled into one. He has always been there in the background, efficient, conscientious, trustworthy. He is a wealthy man in his own right, I believe—ought to be, for his boss had been a minister at Delhi for ten long years. With father gone, baba is now his chaudhuri, and he's started addressing me as such ever since nomination day. Sounded strange at first, but I am getting used to it. A thin, small-made, fair-skinned man when he started off, he is all fleshed out now with a healthy double chin and a respectable midriff, a bundle of energy who combines efficient management with a quiet unobtrusiveness. Essentially a background person. I am glad he's around. In fact, I really don't know what I'd have done without him. I follow his advice blindly, am persuaded to be led where he leads me.

The days are long, fourteen hours at the very minimum. I have three king-sized flasks in my car. One contains iced water; the other has *nimbu pani* laced liberally with salt. The third has hot water for gargles when the throat threatens to give way, the best antidote still for laryngitis. And laryngitis is part of the travails, especially when you have to make between fifteen and twenty speeches a day, a couple of them organized occasions, the rest impromptu, on the spot. A Pentecostish feeling comes on me once in a while as I address these street-corner gatherings with a group of stragglers listening, a collection of random adults, urchins with little better to do, a stray dog or two, the audience busy scratching armpits and groins, digging noses, a few curious, the rest with bored, resigned expressions.

This morning, it is a whistle-stop tour through a cluster of eight villages, I am told, involving a total drive of forty kilometres. My creativity has run itself out some time back. It is almost like pressing a button when I stand in front of a crowd. The words come out robotlike.

'Brothers and sisters. It is the first time that I am coming in your midst. It is an event of untold sadness that has caused me to be here. You all loved my respected father, Chaudhary Raghbir Singh. The affection that he had in his heart for you knew no bounds. But alas, he is no more. It was his last wish that I take his place, that I continue to serve you as he did for over twenty years.' I am not so sure about this last part. He hadn't ever spoken to me about it. But Mummy swears he did, to her. I have to believe her. 'If you search within your hearts, you will know for yourselves how well he has served you, how much he cared for your well-being. He is no more, but his spirit lingers on. I can feel his presence beside me even as I stand here before you. He is the one who gives me strength to take his place, to carry on his good work.'

The last bit is emotional, high-pitched. Pause for dramatic effect. My pyjamas have stopped trying to fall off me, thank goodness. The string doesn't bite any more, for I have discovered the optimum knotting technique through trial and error. I've lost weight in any case. Small mercies. Usha will be pleased with that, at least. 'Today, some people, in the name of religion, others in the name of caste, are out to tear this country asunder, to destroy it. They are trying, but I have confidence that sensible patriots like you will never fall prey to their evil designs. They are people who use divisiveness for mean, narrow political ends. Ours is the party of Gandhiji, of Nehruji, of Indiraji, of Rajivji. It is only we who can keep the country united, provide a stable government. I ask you to vote for all that they and beloved Choudharyji stood for. Jai Hind.'

Not bad going for a first-timer, right? Written out in English, translated carefully, mugged by heart. Three variations. And anything else that Chatar Lal ji wants me to touch upon, venue specific. The cronies chant, the three-car loads that are part of my cavalcade. They always mix with the crowds, lead the hand claps.

The terrain we drive through is parched, brown, dusky. There is no hint of green, for the monsoon is yet to blow in. The only exception to this continuous expanse of grey-brown are the clusters of trees around the villages that stand out as you drive along, like oases in a desert. The loo blows relentlessly, dries your face up to the likes of parchment. Yet by the first week, my body has slowly started to adjust. Thank God I'd kept up my jogging this past year, two rounds of Lodhi Gardens five days a week. And I've discovered what dietary cycle suits this routine the best. Just fruits and buttermilk in the morning, a sandwich for lunch. Lots of fluids in between. And ensconced deep inside our ancestral abode, a couple of large scotch-sodas at night and a reasonably heavy repast afterwards. Not the most healthy of dietary prescriptions, but my routine is hardly normal. Seems to suit me the best for now. Mummy frowns at the alcohol, for politicians aren't supposed to imbibe. There are only a handful who actually don't. Of that I am sure. The old man loved his couple of tots in the evening. But you have to do it in secret, far away from the public eye. Awfully bad form otherwise. I conform.

And the days pass by, in a series of slow-motion frames, or so it seems to me. *Stop feeling sorry for yourself. No one forced you into this. Don't fool yourself into pretending that you didn't have a choice. In the end you did volunteer, didn't you?* Lecturing to myself is easy. It is the physical part that is the toughest still. As the finale nears, the pace is frenetic, a helter-skelter hundred-meter dash, the tape in front of me, yet tantalizingly far. And the competition is catching up, turning the heat on, pouring the money in. Preparations are on in earnest for the final phase. Mummy and Chatar Lal ji take over. I stay out of direct involvement, watch from the sidelines. They seem to know every pocket, every street, all aspects of the political topography.

The last two days are at fast-forward, the pace so frenetic that I haven't even the time to feel sorry for myself. And it's in the middle of all this, on the day before campaigning ends, that Mummy decides to catch up with the unspoken agenda that's been floating around, physically absent, which made it all the worse. 'You'll learn as you go along, baba, you'll learn.' I told you about this tendency of hers to repeat herself. 'You must. Who knows, I may not be around the next time.'

Mummy loves her bit of melodrama. I am the dutiful son for the duration, and I respond as she expects me to be.

'Oh come on, Mummy! You'll live to be a hundred if you live a day.'

I don't know how much Usha would like that.

'Maybe I will, maybe I won't. But the next time around, you are on your own. This time, everything has been so sudden. That's why I am here to help. But let me tell you, I was here every single time with Pitaji. Stayed here with him from the first day to the last. Not like some other people.'

'Be patient, Mummy,' I tell her. 'Usha will adjust. It's been all too sudden for her too.'

This is what happens when you choose your own wife, as un-bahu as they come, no *pallu*-covered head, jeans instead.

'I do hope she does.' Mummy isn't going to let go. Not that easily. 'You've got to be in it together, you know. Together. That much I'm sure of, after being married to your Pitaji for forty years. You've got to have support, you need someone to confide in. Not that he ever used to listen to my advice or even ask me for it. But you've got to be there all the same.'

'We'll talk about it, Mummy,' I tell her. 'Let's get through the next two days first.'

And election day comes and goes. I am out the whole day, going around the district town to just about every booth, grinning and namasteing so relentlessly that my jaws ache gloriously by evening, as do my elbows and my forearms. And my shoulders. And my feet. Chatar Lal ji's arrangements have been near flawless. There have been no incidents except a couple of minor scuffles, induced more probably by the heat and the dust than by anything else. By late night, my state is such that I truly couldn't have cared if I won or lost. My third whisky and Mummy is frowning at me. I've left strict instructions not to be disturbed. My phalanx seemed to be upbeat when I left them. 'You're sure to win,' they said. 'Hands down.' Maybe they have their own methods of exit polling, however crude or seemingly unscientific. I believe them; at least I want to.

Counting starts at the nine the next morning and proceeds at a leisurely pace. Chatar Lal ji's coverage is good. Messages float in fast and furious as the hours go by.

It is near twelve in the afternoon when the first firm trend emerges. Trailing by three thousand. My heart sinks. Yet Chatar Lal ji seems unperturbed. He knows the area to which the booths belong, whose votes have been counted. It has a history of voting against the old man, perhaps some grouse, real or imagined, that the populace holds.

'This is almost a tradition during each election. The first results to come in are always from the Lalpura area, and each time, the trend is the same. Late Chaudharyji was so used to it he used to call it his good omen—this first report that he is trailing. Don't worry. Chaudharyji, we will catch up.'

But no, this time around, the patterns are different. By late afternoon, two thousand have been added to the figure; by half past five, the gap is nine thousand. The Ram bhakt is in the lead. The Mandir strategy seems to be paying off. Now I am truly jittery, for at this stage 90 per cent of the votes have been counted. Only thirty thousand remain. Yet Chatar Lal ji seems unruffled. May be he doesn't want to upset me in advance; maybe he wants me to absorb defeat in slow doses.

Mummy has ensconced herself in an inner room of the outhouse of our ancestral home. The small three-room building serves as my election office. I go in to meet her and express my misgivings. She is sitting cross-legged on a charpoy, the rope sagging beneath her not-inconsiderable weight.

'Don't worry, baba. Don't worry. You'll win. Much closer than I thought it would be, but you'll win.'

How is she so smug, I ask myself, *so sure of herself?* And Chatar Lalji too. Cool, unperturbed. I mean, I am nine thousand behind, and there are only thirty thousand more to be counted. That means I need to get at least twenty of the thirty to even win by a thousand. And the way the trends have emerged, the way I've seen the voting patterns taking shape, no way that can happen. I'm a computer whizz, after all, or was one until recently, and not for nothing.

A half hour goes by; the first ten thousand are through. The message comes, and I have nine thousand of them. Ninety per cent? I can't believe this. Incomprehensible by all counts of logic. *Must be really devoted to the old man*, I tell myself. From eight behind, I am almost level, just a thousand behind. But there's another twenty left, and anything can happen. Rather like the slog over in a one-day match, three wickets in hand, five over remaining, thirty runs to win. A run a ball. Six years in the cricketless United States and I am still an avid fan.

The next ten, and I have seven of them. *This is impossible*, I tell myself. But there it is. I am three up. Wow, I might win even. It is another hour before the final count is done. My nails are chewed down almost to the cuticles. The results come in, and I have twenty-four of the final thirty-two. Scraped through, yes, but I've won! I rush inside to my mother. She gets up to embrace me. Smiling. Triumphant. That is when I smell a rat. Something was up with the last thirty-two thousand. Something more than the devotion of the populace. How could she have been so sure and Chatar Lal ji so complacent? I look her straight in the eye.

'Tell me the truth, Mummy, how did that last count go so lopsided? How did you know with such certainty? There is something to all this that you aren't telling me.'

Mummy preens herself, draws herself up to her full height, all of five feet two.

'You'll learn, baba. In course of time, you'll learn. There is a lot to learn in this game, I can assure you.'

Outside on the courtyard, it is nearing twilight. The crowds are gathering as the news spreads. My cheer leaders start the chant.

'Chaudhary Rajiv Singh, zindabad. Chaudhary Raghbir Singh, amar rahe.'

'Go, baba,' Mummy says. 'They are waiting for you.'

I bend down to touch her feet, and she blesses me, her hand on my head. I walk past her towards the door, on my way out to the courtyard, to lay claim to my inheritance.

* * *

AND LENIN TOPPLES

ffliction. Affectation. Tough choice of word, if you ask me. Difficult to decide which one applies, especially when you are referring to yourself. Honesty can be a painful exercise. The one implies a natural occurrence, something that happens with inevitability to some people; the other conveys shades of hypocrisy, of put-on, of seeming to be something you are not. Let me risk being candid. In my case, it was indeed an affectation. No use denying it. A convenient one at that. It got me into the in-crowd, the crowd that had the prettiest birds. It also provided ample opportunity to while away my time in lively company, especially when I was in danger of experiencing boredom. And yes, admittedly, the conversations were stimulating. I quite enjoyed that part of it. I love a good, rumbustious, no-holds-barred argument even now. But if you ask me, did I believe, did I feel deep within for the Cause, I have to say no. In all honesty. I can, I suppose, afford to now. It's so far back in time. Nothing to lose.

But with some of the others, it was different. For them the credo transcended intellect, went well beyond being in the nature of mere political thinking. Take Kumar, for instance. Ardent belief is an understatement. His whole life seemed to be inextricably woven into the web of Marxian thought. He lived Marx; he breathed Marx. Maybe he dreamt Marx too. And he spouted Marx every moment awake. Kumar of the gaunt face and lanky frame, of the faded blue jeans, of the crumpled white kurta. Of the thick black shock of hair a little too long to be fashionable even in those days of the flower children, ever a shade unkempt. Of the haunting eyes, the Arafat-like three-day stubble. Of the rubber chappals, blue straps on a slightly dirty white base. Of the cotton jhola hanging low and loose from his left shoulder, strands of thread come astray at its seams. Kumar, whose role models of the day were Kanu and Charu, and who but for reasons of geographical non-proximity and parental pressure to graduate would of course have been a part of the movement, sneaking bombs into Calcutta, knifing policemen, doing the hatchet job on kulaks who richly deserved even worse. Or so he said. And he said a lot, all the time. And said it with fluency, with candour, with disarming wit, with an amazing breadth of vocabulary. His accent, of course, was Indian public school, for it was in one of those that he had, though for no fault of his, definitely not out of his choice, been confined as a boarder for many years, a fact that he tried to live down rather desperately but couldn't manage to, for habits and mannerisms die hard, though reason and intellect might demand differently.

With Kumar, let me confirm, it was an affliction. Chronic. Had got him good and proper. That much was obvious. Revolution, he used to say. India was more than ripe for it. Witness the class divide. Look at the poverty. Look at the abject lack of hope the rural poor experienced. Look at the aeons of subjugation, the centuries of intellectual and physical oppression. The whole system stank. And independence hadn't brought any succour, had only worsened matters as corrupt politicians subverted whatever a revisionist government tried to do in its own misguided way. Revolution, Kumar used to say, was only a matter of time. And that is where people like us came in, for we would be the spearheads; we would provide the cutting edge.

I remember that Saturday afternoon vividly, for it was a rainy April day, which for that month was unusual for Madras. There were around ten of us clustered in one corner of the canteen, which we had to ourselves at that time of day. Rohini was there, which was one of the main reasons for my being there too. Rohini was slim and pristine, hair pulled firmly off her well-shaped forehead, tied into a tight knot just above her slender neck. An outsized bindi. A cotton sari of quiet pastel, for that was what went with our crowd. Crisp and starched of course— her Marxism didn't extend to looking shabby. Bright large eyes that sparkled and shone as the conversation flowed. Rohini, who tried hard to look sexless but was only all the more sexy for her efforts. To me, that is. Shades of my Sriram to her Bharati, for I had just that week read *Waiting for the Mahatma*. Walk hand in hand into the sunset.

The arguments stretched late into the afternoon. Endless cups of tea, saucers filled with cigarette butts. And a sneaked joint once in a while. Marijuana and Marxist rhetoric had much in common. Both elevated the spirit. Both set minds free. And loosened tongues. The Russians, we all agreed, were decidedly revisionist. The question was of mainland China. Kumar felt that they had strayed from the purity, the true integrity of the Marxist–Leninist path. Strayed badly, Mao or no Mao. Albania, he said, was the last of the bastions. All strength to Enver Hoxha! And as for India, Naxalbari was just the first seed sown. In Kerala and in Andhra, the violent, relentless winds of change had started to blow. What was needed now was focused activism, widespread propagation. A goading of those teeming millions of the helpless, the downtrodden, into the volatility of action. Revolution! Kumar was fairly bubbling over with excitement, with enthusiasm. He turned to me.

'I am going,' he said. 'A week at home and I am going.'

These were our last couple of days together in college, which is why proximity to Rohini was essential. I had to get to know of her plans. I simply had to.

'Where to?' I asked Kumar.

'To Telengana. I met Nageshwara Reddy last night, do you know? Here, in Madras. I can't tell you where. Too dangerous. I have been sworn to secrecy. But I have arranged to join him. Ten days from now. And he wants more guys like me. Which of you is willing to come with me?'

He looked around at the guys, me included. No takers. Problems at home. Admissions to be sought. Only Rohini volunteered.

'No, Rohini, I can't. Only guys. They were clear about that. This stuff is too dangerous. Maybe later. Come on, tell me, are none of you willing?'

No one looked him in the eye. Kumar's anger boiled over.

'You charlatans!' he yelled, as always, eloquent. 'You mountebanks! You pretenders! You gutless bastards! I can't believe this. Doesn't even one of you have the commitment? It's a question of guts finally, I suppose. Of courage. Cowards!'

And Kumar stalked out, hair ruffled, eyes blazing with righteous rage, arms akimbo as he got that last expletive in. And that was the end of me and Rohini too. Whatever chances I had evaporated into thin air.

That was the last I saw of him before we left college. I often wondered over the years of what could have happened to him. No, he wasn't in politics; at least he wasn't important enough to be reported in the press. Maybe he was a subversive, still in the Telengana jungles, ever on the run, kidnapping village officials every other day and MLAs once in a while. Maybe he was a social worker in some obscure, undeveloped belt, patiently backing propaganda with good deeds and hard work. May be he was in some jail or the other, serving a prolonged sentence for one of the varied acts of violence that he had always threatened to perpetrate. But he was one of the truly afflicted varieties. Of that I was sure.

Not like me. A wife and two kids, a flat on Pedder Road, an air-conditioned Contessa, a Diner's Card. And five stars whilst travelling on work. Four thousand–odd for a meal and a night's repose. That makes even a severely lapsed leftist like me feel guilty. That is where I am now, up on the tenth floor of this towering structure, cocooned in luxury, the remote control of the room TV placed next to me on the bed, lounging around, watching CNN. It is late August, and the coup that failed has just got over. The world is agog with Russia, and CNN is full of it and little else. Gorbachev in a pullover and trousers, conversing with newsmen at his Crimean dacha before he departs for Moscow, his face reflecting relief, yet looking as if he is wondering deep inside whether he had actually won or lost out. Yeltsin, hands raised above his head in confident victory, speaking to a gargantuan throng outside what the anchor terms the Russian White House. The conquering hero. Cheerful scenes of jubilation from the streets of Moscow, guitars playing, people dancing. Interviews with dozens of leaders from the West, each of who proclaims that he always knew that the coup would fail, that the people would triumph.

This is my second day in Delhi on this visit. I leave tomorrow for Bombay in the evening. The day hasn't been a very hard one, and I am in a relaxed frame of mind. But I am bored. You can only take in that much of CNN. And I hate video. As for DD, the less said, the better. I have a troublesome decision to take. Catch 22. Do I order dinner up, or do I go down to one of the restaurants and eat? Room service menus are so standard, I tell myself. All hotels have the same boring stuff, named differently, of course, and described exotically. Creative writing at its best. They all taste the same in the end. But going down is even worse. Eating alone in a restaurant gets me, especially those fifteen or twenty minutes between ordering and being served, when I am unsure of what to do with myself, of where to look, of where to place my hands. On the table or on my lap? I normally keep alternating furiously. The debate takes a while, lubricated with whisky from my hip flask and soda from the tiny fridge tucked into the clothes cupboard. The decision finally made, I splash some water on my face, struggle out of my pyjamas and into my clothes and make my way down to the lobby. Point of decision once again. The coffee shop? Or where else? I decide on a place that serves up some excellent North-West Frontier fare. That, I believe, is the right terminology.

'Do you have a table booked, sir?'

The steward is an intimidating bloke, a tall, imposing figure with a moustache that twirls up majestically at the ends, dressed in stylized Pathan clothing set off with a deep-red waistcoat embroidered with gold braid.

'No,' I tell him. 'I am staying here. I didn't bother to book.' I jingle my room keys.

Hotel guests—I've never figured out why they bill us so extravagantly and yet use that term—are always treated with elaborate courtesy.

'We are full right now, sir, but a table will be free in about ten minutes. Would you like to wait at the bar and have a drink in the meanwhile?'

The bar referred to is conveniently placed at the entrance to the restaurant, a little to the side. Good business strategy. I am browsing over yet another whisky soda, lost in thought, when someone taps me on the shoulder.

'Hi, Rahul, old boy. What a surprise!'

I look up to see a man standing next to me, face crinkled in a smile of recognition, of genuine warmth. I can't quite figure out who he is, though surely I have met him someplace before.

'Hello,' I reply, standing up. 'Sorry, but I can't quite place you.'

'Oh, come on, try,' he says, grinning. 'Surely you can't have forgotten me that easily.'

The individual is around my age, fair and good looking, sleek black hair combed off a broad brow, a face that confesses to good living yet not in the least bit flabby. He is dressed impeccably in a striped shirt, trousers that fit well, polished shoes. By his side is a petite, good-looking woman. I look at him a little more carefully. The features fall into place, a human jigsaw. *It can't be*, I tell myself. Commie Kumar! The cheeks and jawline have filled out; the three-day stubble has given way to a clean, close shave. The unruly hair is well groomed. Kumar, all right.

'Kumar,' I say to him. 'Isn't that right?'

'Right on,' he says. 'Right on. Waiting for someone?'

'No. There wasn't a table free. I'm waiting for one to get vacant.'

'Then you must dine with us. Absolutely. I insist.'

I protest, not wanting to intrude on their evening, but I am persuaded in the end. We are ushered in. Kumar talks in an aside to the steward. An extra place is arranged double quick on their table that is already booked and we sit down. Kumar seems entirely at home in the surroundings. He is a favoured customer and a frequent one, I can see, for the steward and the waiters are ever so deferential to him. The meal that he takes upon himself to order for us is exquisite, and I compliment him on his choice of dishes. Quite the man of the world, accustomed to this ambience of elegance and luxury. As the evening progresses, we catch up.

From the college in Madras to Delhi and JNU for his master's. Soon after, he had joined an advertising agency as a copywriter. He had worked his way up through his fourth job hop in the manner of all good ad folk when he had felt this urge within to launch out on his own.

'That's when I started this small agency, Images. Ever heard of it?'

I had. Images was one of the better-known medium-sized firms, new but very successful. And very competent too, judging from whatever I had seen of their campaigns.

'Yes,' I tell him. 'I am familiar with some of the work your outfit has done.'

'But of course you must be, since you are into consumer-durable marketing yourself. We started off small, but I managed to get a good group of people. Creativity is all in advertising, you know. The rest of it sort of takes care of itself. Or Ila does, in our case.' He nods at his wife.

'I'm no good at the administrative stuff,' he continues. 'But we've had a pretty good run of campaigns. And some good accounts. Haven't lost a single customer to date. It's almost five years into time now since we started off. Ten crores in billing. Pretty good, what?'

I don't believe Kumar was showing off. Or boasting. He'd done well. A self-made man. And he was merely sharing the joy of his success with me, an old friend from days long past. We had a slow, lazy meal, Kumar dominating the conversation as usual. He spoke of his initial struggle in this highly competitive field when accounts were hard to come by. And then the break: with a fledgling consumer durable company, whose work he had accepted for want of not much else coming his way. The brilliant campaign that followed, now a part of advertising folklore. And then the floodgates opened.

After the meal, we shift to the bar, this time a larger one with a TV set. CNN again. Cognac swirls amber and gold in our goblets as Kumar continues to hold forth. As effortlessly articulate as ever, the sentences flow as he speaks of his plans for the future. The bar is well populated, mostly visitors from foreign shores, well-dressed ones, obviously from the west. Dowdy clothes invariably give away the Iron Curtain varieties. Suddenly, the place quietens down. We sense something happening and see all eyes on the TV in the corner, a large thirty-six-incher Sony, the image crystal clear. Live from the USSR, says CNN, a momentous event about to take place. The camera switches to a city square where a giant crane is parked near an oversized statue. Cables tie the statue to the crane's hoist. At an unseen signal, the process of lifting starts. The statue is torn off the pedestal, balances precariously at its edge before it is lifted off it completely. The camera pans in. Lenin's face looms large, unseeing, unperturbed. I glance out of the corner of my eye at Kumar. And he is too. Unperturbed. He turns once again to me. 'With a little bit of luck,' he says, 'I should be doubling next year. Twenty crores. The big league. Wouldn't that really be something?'

⚬ ⚬ ⚬

THE HAND

*S*he can feel what is coming in her bones. Very distinctly.

Yet who is she to blame but herself? The inexorability of it all, the seemingly steady movement at an even, sometimes languid, pace towards a defined end as in a Greek tragedy. Almost as if it was foretold, all of it, as if it was waiting to happen. Her inner desperation is getting to be difficult to conceal anymore, though her stiff upper lip hasn't sagged, not just yet. But it would any day now, with only a couple of months left to the time of reckoning when the knockout punch would be delivered, a clean uppercut that cleaves her chin, leaving her spreadeagled on the floor, dishevelled, immodest, oblivious to the world around her.

And when she wakes, much later, she will be alone and frightened. The hangers-on, the coterie, as the press love to term it, the now fawning sycophants, the gatekeepers would all have fled except perhaps the most ineffectual who would perhaps cling to some thread of misplaced hope. But of what use would they be anyway? Hindsight tells her that it may have been better for her to have stayed aloof, silent, regal, above the rabble and the noise, even though she didn't have her mother-in-law's imperious nose to look down along. Yet she does realize that even such a stance of studied apathy wouldn't last, would lead ultimately to the same piteous finale when the floodgates would open, when the past would come rushing at her like angry dark monsoon clouds, drenching her, leaving her and her children deprived of the last shreds of dignity.

It was for the two of them that she had tried, for she lived only for them now that he had departed. She berated herself constantly for having let all this come to such a pass. If only she had put her foot down very firmly when he was first pushed into stepping into this sordid new world of politics and governance, maybe she might have been able to stop him, and then their existence would have been so different. The four of them together, cosy, finding in each other love, contentment, strength, happiness.

She shudders at the thought of the thankless ordeal that confronts her, dreary, tiresome days full of frenetic movement from one bleak spot to the next. The raised platforms of rattling planks held precariously together with bamboo and rope. The crowds that stare up at her, a faceless mass, some brought in with inducements, some present out of curiosity. The dust, the heat, the flies, the omnipresent underlay of sweat and grime. The unpleasant melange of smells that had almost sent her into a faint the first time around, now evoking feelings that are a mixture of fortitude and distaste. And the same banal words uttered in a language that she can comprehend and articulate after these many years but knows she can't ever be fluent in.

Contrast, she tells herself, the low, misty hills of Franconia, the countryside around Nuremberg where she grew up. The thick green hedges, the low grass-swept hills, the winding country roads that she used to cycle on, the church spires that peeped out from amongst clusters of houses, the ivy-covered cottages with their pretty gardens. The deep, orderly dark forests of tall pine. And snaking through in a sweeping curve, the six lanes of the autobahn. Maybe that is where they might have gone to live, the four of them, if this perilous path hadn't been chosen.

She is dressed for the morning in a starched pastel sari worn over a thick blouse a shade darker in colour. The blouse has sleeves to the elbow and buttons up to the neck. The *pallu* is positioned such that it can be turned up easily to cover her head without ruffling her tightly combed head of thick brown hair. Her feet are encased in sensible thick-soled, buckled sandals of soft leather, designed for the wear and tear of the frantic times ahead.

Kalu Ram has her breakfast ready, a bowl of freshly sliced red-orange papaya to be washed down with a glass of cold milk. It is as she is finishing the last of the milk that she notices Kalu Ram by her side, scratching the behind of his head diffidently, wanting obviously to say something, conveying by his actions that he is not certain whether he should. She smiles at him and says, 'Go on, Kalu, what is it?'

Affection is palpable in her voice for Kalu has been the one through the past five years, with her children away at college overseas. Through this period of uncertainty and upheaval, he has been there, silent and unobtrusive. Always.

'I have brought someone,' he says. 'I want you to spend time with him.'

'Who is it?'

'A baba who had come to see me. Last week. When I was at home.'

Kalu Ram had been gone a week, up into the Kumaon hills where he belonged, from where —as he liked to tell her—the eternal, mystical snows of the sacred peaks were seemingly only an arm's length away.

'Now what do I need with a baba, Kalu?' she asks. 'I have enough troubles in front of me as it is without anyone adding to the confusion.'

'Precisely for that, madam. For your troubles. Maybe he can help. Just spare him a minute. If what he says makes sense, you can see him once again. In the evening.'

She nods, a little reluctantly. *Trust Kalu*, she tells herself. To take his baba past the Z security cordon that was an inescapable part of her life.

He comes back almost immediately, the baba in tow.

Not her image of what a baba ought to look like—no tangled beard, no matted hair, no ashes that cover the forehead. Instead a dapper, spare person of medium height, long hair pulled back and tied into a tight bun at the nape of his neck, much like her own, an orderly thick black beard, a deep red spot of sindoor just above where his eyebrows meet. He is dressed in a neat white kurta pyjama, and as he folds his palms in a namaste, she notices that his eyes are his most distinctive feature, for it is as if they pierce through her as they sparkle and shine.

'The hand, *mataji*. The lines on the palm. They are all wrong. Let me draw them out for you. And you will win. I promise you that.'

She does not comprehend for just a moment. And then the context dawns on her, and she smiles at him. *Why not?* she tells herself. *Won't do any harm, in any case.*

'Draw them for me,' she says, 'and explain them to me. Then we will see.'

'It is ready with me, *mataji*.' He unrolls a broad sheet of thick white paper that he is carrying with him.

'In the evening,' she tells him. 'When I have more time.'

It is a long day, endless confabulations with a bewildering variety of individuals, all clad in white, as if cloned for the occasion. And an equally bewildering variety of languages and dialects. This is the season for distribution of tickets to contest, a messy job at best, impossible at most times. She is tired, both physically and in the mind. She has had little time to dwell on the encounter of the morning, and the couple of times that she does think about it, she is unsure. Of whether to laugh the whole thing off or to actually spend time with Kalu's baba. Now she is washed and changed and ready for dinner, a place set for one at the head of the table. She decides. *No harm done*, she says to herself. Yet the part of her that still belongs to Deutschland sniggers. But only gently.

After the meal, Kalu and the baba come in.

'I will keep it brief,' he tells her. 'You look tired.'

He unrolls the paper and places an unused spoon on one side of it, a fork on the other so that the paper lies flat and taut. The hand looks to be the same as the one in the posters at the party's central office; at least it looks familiar. And within the palm, neatly drawn, are the lines. The baba explains.

'The lifeline,' he says, 'is unbroken and of even texture. It skirts the mount of Venus in a gentle curve while staying close to it. And it ends into the first *rascette* on the wrist, joins it and travels along with it. This is how the line ought to be. It is indicative of a combination of long life, peace, and success.

'The head line is joined to the life line at the start but separates soon thereafter. If they remain joined for too long, it is not a good sign. It would signify a lack of self-confidence. And the line travels in a gentle curve that skirts Uranus and at the termination is taut and straight. A combination of high degrees of intelligence and common sense. And the heart line starts with a fork deep within Jupiter and traverses the entire length of the hand spaced just the right distance away from the line of head. What it indicates is a combination of success and graciousness.

'The line of Saturn, of course, commences in Luna and terminates at the centre of its mother mount. The best indication possible. And the sun line too runs sure, straight and uncut rising in the middle of the palm and ending into the right higher, signifying glorious success, as glorious as the sun god himself. And finally the line of Mercury, indicative of both health and wealth, which rises long straight from Luna, ending up at the base of the little finger.

'This,' the baba tells her, 'is as good as you can get. With lines such as these, there is no way that you can lose. Victory, and a thumping one at that, is assured.'

He finishes, and he looks up at her, and those disconcerting eyes peer once again as if into the depths of her soul. And to her side is Kalu Ram, looking a little nervous as he scratches the back of his head once again.

Her mind is suddenly made up. She stands up and says namaste to the baba. She goes into her bedroom and comes back with two five hundred rupee notes that she offers him. But 'No,' he says. 'All I want is that what I have given you works. And you win.' He is firm. She relents. And as Kalu escorts his guest out, she can see Kalu smiling to himself, satisfied.

If there is one thing about the organization that she heads that makes her happy, it is the quality of compliance to instructions from the very top. Within days, photocopies of the baba's drawing of the hand are with every functionary that counts. What madam says goes. And so the posters are printed in their thousands with the lines on the palm as the baba had drawn them. No questions are asked as to where the drawing has come from. Madam wants it this way. And so it must be done.

From the depths of despondency to a willingness to engage in battle. From diffidence to increasing degrees of self-belief. From being cajoled into action to storm trooping from the front. She is amazed at the fount of energy that she discovers within herself. And even more amazing is the transformation that the moribund party of hers undergoes. Togetherness and teamwork in a set-up where attempting to lynch one another is a regular pastime. Of ensuring each candidate's victory instead of clandestine undermining. Hard work and campaigning that stretches late into the night instead of a Patiala at twilight.

* * *

Excerpts from *The Leader of the National Age*

15 November 2002

Never in its fifty years of existence has the country witnessed a transformation in electoral fortunes as dramatic as this. From being an underdog, written off several times over, the . . . Party under the leadership of Ms — has achieved the unbelievable. A two third majority in Parliament. And not only that, a mandate that is truly national in its nature. There is no single state of the union that has not returned the party with a thumping majority. In fact, in psephological terms, the voting patterns are almost eerily uniform from province to province.

The irony of what has happened cannot be forgotten. That fifty years after the last Englishman who ruled us left our shores, a daughter of Europe was sworn in as prime minister last evening.

* * *

A GUFFAW IN THE END

*Y*es, Mrs Malhotra said to herself as she opened the night latch on the door and let herself into the two-bedroom DDA that was her home, weddings are expensive and getting more so with each passing year. If you tot up all the stuff, if you account for every pin and needle, the figures are enough to make you feel faint. A large sum in cash is a given nowadays, solid hard cash in an FD in the girl's name, enough to earn adequate interest to supplement the happy couple's income and make frills and fancies affordable. And that is just the beginning of a long, expensive list. A factory-fresh sedan is an absolute must, the Honda Civic the current favourite. Then the clothes—enough to start a small store with. Suits, the pinstriped variety for the gents, ethnic designer stuff for the ladies, skirts for the little girls, baba suits for the male versions. For the families on both sides, mind you. The wider the coverage, the better. Cousins and in-laws on the boy's side can earn you great goodwill. Goodwill that lasts, for when you visit cousins in Punjabi Bagh and you see a Mahila Society mob outside some house holding a protest, you feel slightly queasy. No, this wouldn't happen to Asha; I am sure it wouldn't. But what is the guarantee? What guarantee that after all the bargaining is over and the marriage itself, no fresh pressures would come? No, no guarantee, just trust in fate and God and everything else that makes things go right, no other surety, especially if what she is going into is a large family, all living together. A mother-in-law in the same dwelling as her accentuates the fragility of the situation, for antagonism between the husband's mother and the bride is a part of the great subcontinental tradition; and when the conflict has an underpinning of the financial, it can often get to be a shade vicious.

And then of course, the goods. White goods, distributed durables, concept marketing items. A TV is almost compulsory; the larger the screen size, the better. Of late also a stereo system—the boy adores western pop—a washing machine, a vacuum cleaner. Sundry things like steam irons and pop-up toasters. Jewellery, gold, and furniture are inescapable parts of tradition any way. The larger the sums expended, the greater the prestige. Four days of celebrating, some days full-scale like the day of the ceremony and the day before, others at half pace. It all adds up. To quite a bit. But there is nothing you can do about it, Mrs Malhotra says to herself. After all, it is a matter of face. Her husband, an important government servant, now retired but still retaining the halo of once having been senior and of consequence, and Asha, their only girl, their only child, in fact. This was but the least that everyone would expect. Most of them didn't know that the earnings on a government job, even one as senior as deputy secretary, didn't offer much scope for large savings. Especially if you were as scrupulously honest as Mr Malhotra had always been.

Thank God they had applied for a DDA allotment quite some time back. At last they had a reasonable roof over their heads. And years of careful spending had enabled them to put away enough so that there would be something left over for a reasonably comfortable, if constantly careful, existence once Asha was married and gone.

Asha was a chartered accountant. So what if they didn't have a son? Both of them were so proud of her. She has done well for herself, a first in commerce and then both the inter and the finals at the first attempt. She had always been provided the best education possible, and it showed. Imagine, she was earning almost as much as her father had when he was about to retire! Not that this would, in any way, help save on the expenses related to her marriage. That was, after all, a matter of form, a part of the unavoidable. Mrs Malhotra was worried about finding a suitable boy. Asha was a headstrong sort, and the right person, someone acceptable both to them and to her, wasn't going to be easy to come by.

Mrs Malhotra had been out shopping that April morning. Unseasonably hot for April, she thought, as she sipped a glass of cold water and sat herself under the fan in the drawing room of their flat, trying to cool herself off. All was quiet in the apartment. Asha was off to Bombay for a couple of days. She had left early that morning for the airport. Mr Malhotra would be back for lunch any moment now. After retirement, he helped with administrative work with a voluntary organization. Good for him, she always said, to keep himself occupied. She had finished cooking early that morning. The sabzi and dal were ready. She would start rolling the dough for the rotis only after her husband came in, for he liked them right off the fire, hot and fresh. It wouldn't take more than a trice.

Mrs Malhotra couldn't take her mind off her daughter's marital state. She was twenty-four already. Thirty years back, at the time she herself was married, twenty-four was positively old-maidish. Today of course, it wasn't too old. But better get her married fast, she told herself. Waiting too long isn't going to help. Within the year or, latest, early the next. But girls were so different today, so much more independent. They had their own minds and pretty strong ones at that. Take Asha. Despite repeated entreaties, she had said no to the IAS, a no that seemed an air of finality about it. A government job was not for her, she said. Look at her—she had packed a bag last night and was off to Bombay alone, staying there in a hotel! Imagine! I wouldn't ever be able to do that, Mrs Malhotra told herself, not even in my next life. Twenty-four was just the right age. She better act fast. The Kochcher boy was good-looking and a doctor. The family seemed nice, but the demands were steep. The Malhotras could barely afford it; it would make a sharp dent into what would be left over for them to live on. Not that it mattered. Asha's well-being was what counted the most. What did we old people need in any case, she said to herself. A doctor from a good family was worth every rupee spent.

Mrs Malhotra's sister Leela had dropped in the previous afternoon to talk about the Khanna boy. He was an IAS all right but Andhra cadre, posted in some district town with an unpronounceable name. Would Asha be happy in such place, especially down in the south? She doubted it. Besides, the only time she had met the Khannas at a wedding last year, they had seemed more than a little puffed up about their IAS son.

Maybe the Puri boy was the best bet. He was an engineer and an MBA and worked for a computer company at Delhi. But negotiations hadn't progressed any.

Sensing that her husband would be back any moment, she moved to the kitchen and stared moistening the flour for the rotis. It was all very well for him, lecturing her about the evils of the dowry system, but was there any practical way of escaping it? Who would marry Asha without a dowry? And more than anything else, would she ever be able to show her face to her friends and her relatives again if Asha was bid farewell accompanied by anything less than a grand ensemble of goods and, as important, a healthy bank balance? She was their only child, after all. She was still deep in her thoughts when she heard the key turn in the latch on the front door. That was her husband returning. *Must persuade him to accompany me to Leela didi's place this evening*, she said to herself. The Puri boy's case needed some pushing.

'Letter for me?' Mr Malhotra asked, picking up a slim white envelope from the low table at one side of the drawing room.

'I don't think so,' she said. 'I didn't pick up anything from the letter box.'

The letter boxes for all the flats on the floor were in a row on the landing, painted a now-faded olive green, the apartment numbers that had been inscribed in white by now half scratched off by some kid or the other in the block on his way up and down the stairs. She had checked their particular box on the way in, and it had been empty. Mrs Malhotra walked over and peered at the envelope. It just said 'Papa and Mummy'. The handwriting was

Asha's. But why should Asha leave a letter behind? She had departed at half past four after a hasty cup of tea, the bank's pickup car waiting down below to transport her to the airport. Maybe it was something she wanted done in her absence. No, it couldn't be. *In that case she would have told me at least twice over knowing how forgetful I am,* thought Mrs Malhotra. She was still wondering when her husband opened the letter. He read it and handed it over to the without comment. Thank God I was standing near the sofa when I read it, she said to herself later, else I might have collapsed to the ground in a heap and broken a bone or two!

'I am off to Bombay today, but not on work. I am getting married to someone there. His name is Alok Kapur, and he used to be a colleague of mine in Delhi. He and I will return to Delhi tomorrow evening. We will reach around eight. Please don't come to the airport. We'll find our way home. I am sorry to announce things this way, but don't worry unnecessarily. Everything will be fine. Love, Asha.'

The words seemed to leap out of the page and grab at her. Little wonder that Mrs Malhotra's head reeled. Yes, thank God for the sofa. This was every bit worthy of a fainting spell. How could she do this to us? How will we ever show our faces to anyone again? Serves me right, bringing her up the way I did. Encouraging her to work, granting more freedom than a girl her age ought to have been given. And my husband is to blame even more than me. Doting on her, never restraining her. This was bound to happen. But why couldn't she have gone about it properly if she did feel like it? After all, the boy was a Kapur; caste considerations wouldn't have stood in the way. If he were at least as well placed as she was, there wouldn't have been any objections at least, no obvious ones. How could Asha be so callous?

She changed tack. Can we prevent this from happening even now? No, it is too late. How do we get anything moving in Bombay?! Oh! What a shame! How will we ever look anyone in the face again?

She glanced at Mr Malhotra. He seemed strangely serene. That riled her all the more. *Doesn't he feel any sense of responsibility for what has happened? How can he be so calm, so smug, after what has occurred?* 'Why aren't you saying anything at all?' she asked angrily.

Mr Malhotra shrugged his shoulders ever so slightly. 'Asha says that all is well. I don't think there is any cause for worry on her account. Whatever has happened has happened. Let us wait till she gets back before getting worked up or jumping to conclusions.'

'But how can you take this attitude? We don't know where she is. We don't know who the boy is.'

She grew even angrier, even more agitated. It took Mr Malhotra a good half an hour of talking to her to calm her down somewhat, but even then her silence had an underlay of sullen hurt and scepticism.

She'd never ever forgive Asha for this, she said to herself. *She had no right to do this to us. We will never be able to live down the shame this will cause.* And what about her trousseau? She hadn't even gone about buying anything much yet, for she hadn't felt any urgency. How was she to know that something terrible like this would happen? Their only daughter. No, this was just too terrible to accept. *Our only daughter, and we aren't even able to make an occasion of her wedding. What would people say?*

Mrs Malhotra nibbled at her lunch. How could he bring himself to eat so heartily? Mrs Malhotra didn't know how she went through the rest of the day. Very often, she itched to ring up Leela didi, but she restrained herself. Better keep this strictly a secret until Asha comes back and we meet this Alok Kapur or whatever his name is. She didn't trust even Leela didi fully; just maybe she would talk to someone else, and then for sure this shameful episode would be public knowledge in hours. No, she better keep this to herself. She sulked at her husband all day long. He had better share the blame for what has happened. Didn't he experience any affront? How could he accept things so equanimously? He had better confront Asha and this Alok when they get here and give them a piece of his mind. That was his responsibility. Not hers.

Mrs Malhotra slept fitfully that night, her mind a whirl of thoughts and emotions. She was up and about early the next day. She spent half the morning tidying up the small apartment, prettying it up as best as she could. After all, however disillusioned she might be, it was her son-in-law who was coming that evening. They would stay here surely. Asha's bedroom had a double bed already. She spread it neatly. For the two of them. That got her worked up once again. What a shame! What a terrible, unspeakable shame! Wait till she saw her. Whatever her father did or didn't do, she was going to get it from her. Her anger suddenly dissolved into sobs as her anger, her helplessness, came pouring out in tears that wet her dupatta as she wiped her eyes with it.

That's when she remembered that the larder was near empty. No sweets, no savories. And what would she cook for dinner? She went into the bedroom where Mr Malhotra, who hadn't gone to work that day, was lying around in his kurta pyjama, reading a magazine. She hauled him out and sent him to the market with instructions to bring back vegetables and at least a kilo of kaaju burfis, an essential part of the ritual, as the couple walked into the house. She spent most of the afternoon and evening cooking a simple yet superb meal. Now, she said to herself as she changed into fresh clothes that evening, all was ready for their arrival. But what was the point? This was not the way she ever imagined things would happen.

As the hour approached eight that night, her tension grew. She fidgeted, adjusted things around the house, took one last look at Asha's room to make sure that everything was neat. She then stationed herself near the drawing room window from where she could see the street beneath.

It was almost ten past eight when she saw a car stopping, heard two pairs of footsteps climbing up the single flight of stairs that led to their apartment on the first floor, heard the doorbell ring. Mrs Malhotra removed herself to the kitchen and shut the door. She didn't want to face Asha as she came in. She heard her husband being introduced to that man, and then she heard Asha asking her father where Mummy was. Her body tensed as Asha opened the door and came in. Mrs Malhotra found herself weeping for the second time that day, her emotions a mixture of hurt and anger together with relief at seeing Asha. Asha hugged her tight and whispered to her, 'Don't cry, Mummy. Everything is I am back. Come and meet Alok.'

'Why did you do this, Asha?' she asked through her tears. 'Why did you do this to us? If you liked him and he liked you, you could have told us, and we would have talked to his parents. Why did you have to shame us so?'

'Look, Mummy,' she said, 'I knew that you would be upset. Despite that, I knew that I had to do what I did. Alok is nice, I am sure you will like him. As acceptable as anyone you would yourself have found. But let me tell you one thing, Mummy. I want you to enjoy your old age in comfort, not spend the better part of your money that I know is hard-earned, that has taken a lifetime to save. Such a mindless waste . . .'

From the drawing room, she heard her husband guffawing at something Alok had said—quite unlike him, normally.

* * *

Printed in the United States
By Bookmasters